OH, YOU PRETTY THINGS.

By Axl Malton

CHAPTER 1.

Jack put two small suit cases in the boot of the car. He added a blanket and a nappy bag with enough nappies to get through a long weekend. Rusty hinges squealed as he shut the boot lid.

'Right. Who's ready for a holiday!?' Jack yelled as he sat in the driver's seat. He was answered with a resounding cheer of celebration from his two children. He blew warm air into closed fists and rubbed his hands together.

'How far is it daddy?' Penny, Jack's ten-year-old daughter asked.

'Pretty far sweet heart. Scotland is a whole other country.'

Penny slumped in her seat, unable to mask the disappointment of a long journey.

'We'll be there before you know it. Put your seat belt on honey.' Jack said and leant over into the back, checking the harness of the baby seat was secure. An excited giggle and a series of incomprehensible words came from his two-year-old toddler, Benjamin. Or 'Benny' as everyone called him.

'Ra Ra hol-day!' Benny clapped.

'That's right kiddo. Holiday.'

'Dad my seat belt won't go in the buckle. Grrr!' Penny grunted in frustration and let go of the belt, letting it snap back into its holster.

'You just haven't got the knack.' Jack said, keeping calm and keeping smiling. It had been a long time since they had been able to get away, he wasn't going to let this holiday get off to a bad start. He leant over to Penny's side and pulled the belt round her. 'You've got to stick it in, and lever it to the left until you hear a –' There was a sharp *click* sound.

'There you go. Safe and secure.'

Penny flashed an insincere smile. The one she had inherited from her mother, the one used when Jack would reel off a series of unfunny 'dad' jokes. He turned the key in the ignition, the engine choked but failed to fire.

Jack stopped and tried again but nothing happened. He gripped the steering wheel with both hands and took two deep breaths. He closed his eyes, the all too familiar feeling of pressure and parental inadequacies building. He muttered quietly to himself. 'Not now. Get us there, get us back... please let us have this one weekend.' Whether he was praying to a real God or not, he didn't know. No one had answered him before, but there was a first time for everything. A positive mental attitude could take you further than you might think. An attitude *he* had inherited from his wife. He turned the key again, this time the engine fired, a loud *bang* came from the exhaust, a look in the rear-view mirror showed a plume of black smoke. He could live with that. 'Alrighty then. Let's go on holiday.' The cheer that came from the back of the car was only half as enthusiastic as the first time. Penny barely raised her voice. The excitement had been replaced with anxiety. The last time she saw her dad close his eyes and pray to himself like that. Was over her mother's dead body.

***

Winter had come early this year. It was barely the end of October and the temperature had plummeted low enough to give the roads a sheet of black ice. The council's must have been caught out because Jack, Penny and Benny were able to make a game of counting the grit lorries on their way out of the city. The thought crossed Jack's mind that if it was this bad here, how bad would it be when they reached the Loch's in Scotland? He put it to the back of his mind, if there's snow the kids can make a snowman, if it's so cold their fingers and thumbs go numb, they can make a roaring fire in the lodge he had rented. They could toast marsh mallows over the flames like they were camping. Positive thinking can get you through anything, he told himself. He turned on the head lights to account for the surface spray and the dark clouds that stretched from here to forever, and flicked the wipers on to clear the windscreen, sounding somewhat disgruntled about being asked to do their job as they screeched with every swish back and forth.

'Do you know where we're going?' Penny asked worriedly.

'Yes darling, of course I do.'

'We've never been before. What if your phone runs out of

battery?' She pointed to the dash mounted phone with the map highlighting which road to take.

'Relax sweetheart.' Jack leant across and grabbed a folded map. 'I've marked out all the roads we have to take, so if my phone dies, or we run out of signal, I've got the good ol' fashioned way of getting us there. Happy?'

She nodded.

'Is it much further?' Penny asked.

Jack laughed. 'We've only been on the road twenty minutes. Once we're out of the city, the traffic will ease up and we'll be zooming up the A1, putting plenty of road behind us. Ok?'

Penny folded her arms and looked out the window. Jack watched her in the rear-view. It had been a hard time for her. Hard for all of them in truth. He was glad that Benny was too young to understand, too young to be able to miss his mum. Even though he's sure Benny will have lots of questions about his mum when he's older.

A David Bowie song came on the radio, and as quick as the first Chord struck, Jack's arm flashed to the tuning knob and changed the station. He checked the rear-view and saw Penny looking back at him with big sad eyes. She turned back to the window.

A news bulletin came on the radio, a series of dramatic and ominous notes set the tone.

'Sad news today. A young girl has been found dead at the Loch Lomond national park in Scotland. Hikers found her body by the Ben Lomond Mountain peak. Early reports suggest she had been sexually assaulted before being suffocated. She was nine-years-old. Police report that the family have been notified. Early suggestions were that the young girl found was Claire Halliday, who has been missing since New Year's Day, some ten months ago. Police can confirm at this moment, that is not the case.

'Holy Christ.' Jack turned the tuning knob again. Penny didn't look away from her window that time. Jack hopes she was too lost in her own world to take any of that in. He turned back to the station that had no news reports and only played constant music.

Even though it was basically the same playlist played over and over, repeating every four hours or so. The less he heard about that story the better. *Nine-years-old.* He thought to himself. *That could have been Penny.* Horrified by his own thoughts he shook them away. *Happy thoughts and positive thinking.* He repeated over and over in his head until the news story became a distant memory. AC/DC came on the radio. He performed an eccentric duet of 'Highway to Hell' with Bon Scott. Then he forgot all about the murdered girl.

***

The A1 was a long and dull road with little to entertain the kids. Penny was ok, quiet, deep in thought the majority of the time, but in generally good spirits. She played the 'I spy' games and sang 'Old Macdonald had a farm.' Benny loved the E-I-E-I-O parts. The only parts he could sing along with. Benny started to get restless so they stopped at a service station after the Leeds sign and before the York sign. Jack changed Benny's nappy before lunch. They grabbed a burger from the Burger King. Jack had the Aberdeen Angus and got the kids the Burger King equivalent of a happy meal. After eating, Jack got Benny a toy from the vending machines for a pound. It was a small plastic tractor that probably cost the company all of five pence to produce. It entertained Benny and kept him contentedly quiet, so that was all that mattered. Penny was content with just getting on with the drive. She didn't know where they were going in Scotland yet, Jack was saving that for a surprise.

They got back on the motorway, the surface spray got so bad north of Leeds that all three lanes were filled with hovering red fog lights and, much to Penny's annoyance, the speed limit dipped from a steady seventy to fifty.

'This is so boring. Are we even halfway yet?' She snapped.

'When we go past the angel, we'll be halfway.'

'What angel?'

'The angel of the North. You'll know when you see it.'

By the time they reached the great metal sculpture, Benny

had fallen asleep, plastic toy tractor present and accounted for in his small bunched up fist.

'There!' Jack pointed to a line of pine trees that stood in front of the statue.

'Oh yeah…Cool.' Penny said unimpressed, and sat back in her seat.

'You know how high that thing is? 66 feet. It's wing span is 177 feet. It took four years to build.' He looked at her in the rear-view and saw no change in her appreciation for it. Dejected, he said: 'It's supposed to create a sense of embrace. Like it's watching over us.' Penny's face didn't change. She carried on staring out of the window, watching the men in high-vis jackets battle the winter elements to complete the never-ending road improvements.

'Do you think Mummy's watching over us?' She said, her voice soft.

Jack found he was spending more time looking at the rear-view mirror than he was at the road.

'Yes. I believe she is darling.'

'Is she an angel now?'

'What do you think?'

'I think she is. I think she's a beautiful angel. Even more beautiful than when she was with us. And a million times more beautiful than that thing.'

Jack smiled at that.

***

'1…2…3! Welcome to Scotland!' All three of them shouted as they crossed the border. Even Benny was able to join in, having woke from his nap refreshed and in a jovial mood.

'Not far now guys. And don't worry about the weather. It's only going to make our time here even more magical.' The first flutter of snowflakes had begun to fall and land on the windscreen. The sky wasn't black, but deep grey and moody. The clouds looked thick and full of snow. The higher they got as they drove through the Scottish Highlands, the closer the clouds seemed to be and the heavier the snow fell.

'Is there a Loch where we're staying?' Penny asked. She knew about Loch's because of the famous Loch Ness monster. They had never been there as a family before, even though Penny had always wanted to.

Jack smiled. 'Maybe.' His smile turned wider when he saw Penny slowly turn her head from the window and look at him.

'Don't you mess with me.' She said, with extra sass. Thanks Billie Eilish or whoever the hell kids are into these days.

'I ain't messin' witchu!' Jack snapped his fingers twice in front of his face and employing a terrible American accent.

'We're going to find Nessie!?'

Jack laughed. 'Don't get your hopes up though. Many have tried and nearly all have failed. But we can certainly have a good look whilst we're there. Who knows, the monster might find us.'

Penny sat back in her seat and looked out the window again. Only this time, she had a great smile on her face that showed off all of her teeth. Benny shouted *NESSIE! NESSIE!* In his own excitement.

The radio crackled with static. 'What the - ?' Jack messed with the tuning knob trying to get the music back on. There was a news reporter giving more information on the murdered girl found at Loch Lomond by the hikers. They had no one in custody. Jack didn't want to hear it, he didn't want to spend his holiday worrying or having bad thoughts. He turned the knob some more, where there would normally be stations all he found was static, as if all signal towers had been destroyed, or someone was jamming the signal. Then the music began playing. It was David bowie again. He was singing 'Oh you pretty things.' Jack shot his hand to the tuning knob then stopped himself.

Jack's memory flashed back to Heather, rocking Benny in one arm and holding Penny in the other, on the arm chair at home she used for night feeding Benny, singing this song to them. He could hear her voice now instead of Bowie's. Sweet and melodic. He pulled his hand away from the radio and let them listen.

When it finished, Penny turned to look at her dad and said:

'You're doing a good job dad.'

He looked back at her with a confused smile. 'Thanks honey.'

As they drove further on and the time passed by, Jack kept checking on Penny in the mirror, and was relieved to see that the smile he had put on her face had seemed to lighten her complexion, the sadness that had been in her eyes seemed to have all but disappeared. Not gone, he didn't think it would ever be totally gone, but if she can find ways of letting joy and happiness outweigh it for the majority of the time, he thinks she'll be alright.

***

By the time they made it to the national Park of Loch Lomond (thankfully they were only passing here and heading north to Loch Ness) the snow was two foot deep either side of the well gritted road. Jack pulled over to consult his map. The kids were being good considering the long drive. Even he was getting tired and frustrated now.

'Are we lost?' Penny asked.

Jack turned the map, tracing his finger along the red line he had drawn over the roads he wanted to take.

'Dad? Are we lost?'

'Lost?' Benny added.

'No, we're not lost.' He folded the map and put it onto the passenger seat. 'I wouldn't need to use this thing if my damn phone had reception. Is it so hard to put 5G towers up here? We have them everywhere else.'

Penny and Benny looked at each other. Penny Shrugged and Benny copied. Then they both laughed. The sound warmed Jack's heart and he reminded himself why he was doing this. He had to make happy memories in their child hood, so when they looked back, they didn't just remember the dark times. It had consumed them for so long. He couldn't, no, he *wouldn't* let it cast a shadow over all their memories. When they were older, they would look back and remember that they had a lot of happy times, more happy than sad. Even though the sad times were the saddest they could ever be and the hardest to think about.

***

They'd been on the road now for seven hours. The sun was setting and with less and less light to help give them some sort of bearing as to where they were in correlation with the map, Jack was rueing the decision to set off at lunch time instead of breakfast. The snow came at them fast and heavy as they drove steadily over the narrow country lanes of the highland mountains. The wipers of Jack's beat up old Ford were working overtime now, but thanks to the thickness of the snow, they did so quietly.

'How is everyone back there?'

'We're ok.' Penny said unconvincingly. She held Benny's hand in hers and stroked his fingers softly, reassuring him. There was something uncanny about children; they were able to sense the tension and fear in an atmosphere, despite not having a clue about any of the context. As far as Benny knew, they were just driving and the snow that was piling higher and higher outside was exciting. The look on his face suggested he was picking up the fear from the energy Jack and Penny were giving off.

'Dad, is the snow ever going to stop?'

'It will do eventually love. We're not far now.' He pulled over into a small lay by. In the summer, he imagined this lay by to be full of tourists, taking in the eye-catching views that being this high up has to offer, the loch's below them, vast hillsides and green land. Polar opposite to now. Now he couldn't see two feet in front of his face. Jack grabbed the map and unfolded it on his knee. He turned the air vent to face the other way, the hot air he had cranked up was making the pages flap as he was trying to read them. 'The map says to go all the way around the mountain and we'll be at the lodge. Another thirty miles or so.'

'How long will that take?' Penny asked.

Jack realised he was conferring with his ten-year-old daughter as if she was an adult. He supposed that was what happened when you were so used to having someone by your side to discuss things with, then when they are taken away from you, you're so stuck with needing someone to run things by, you do it anyway, to whoever will listen. The fact that she's engaging in the conversation and soothing her younger brother to stop him from being frightened means she's done what most kids do when they lose a parent at a young age- they grow up quick.

'I don't know sweetie. An hour, maybe longer with this weather.' He looks at the map again, waiting for an answer to jump out at him. He thinks he's found one. 'Wait...There's a road that goes straight over the mountain, it'll be dangerous, the snow will be higher up there, but it would mean we only had ten miles to travel instead of thirty. It also means we could be there in half an hour (positive thinking)...what do you say?'

Penny looked outside. A huge gust of wind rocked the car, snow pelted the window. The sun disappeared and the world looked like it morphed into nothing. 'I'm scared dad. I just want to get to the house.'
'Straight over the mountain it is then.'

***

The radio was out. The only sound that came from the speakers was static. Jack kept it on with the volume up because he didn't dare take his hands off the wheel or his eyes from the road for a second. He was driving slowly, but the twists and turns this high up were so sharp and treacherous, one wrong move would see them all plummeting down the side of the mountain. He was glad then that he couldn't see. If he could, he would know there was no guard rail, only a sheer drop down the side. The car was struggling on the high snow, hell, this car struggled on well tarmacked city roads, the fact it was still going was nothing short of a miracle.

Maybe there *was* an angel watching over them?

The heat was pumping from the vents and filling the car. The cars thermometer told him the outside temperature was far worse, minus twelve worse.

'I think we're over the worst of it.' Jack said, reassuring himself as much as the kids. He couldn't quite believe they'd managed it, but here they were coming to a clearing -

The car's head lights, that had only so far illuminated each individual snow flake as it fell, now showed a giant rock wall that they were heading straight into. He turned the wheel, the tyres skidded along the compacted snow surface like a skate over ice. Jack pumped the brakes, hoping, praying to God, a real God, a fake one, to anyone that would listen, to let the tyre's catch some friction and power them around the corner and away from the rock wall. His prayers were answered, but not before the car spun 180 degrees. The back end of the car thumped the rock face hard, smashing all the tail lights. The sound of glass shattering made Benny begin to cry and wail. Tears wet his cheeks and snot bubbles burst out of his nose.

'It's ok Benny. It was just a little bump. We'll be ok.' That was Penny. Jack was squeezing the steering wheel so the leather creaked in his palms. He had his eyes closed and was biting his lip. He wanted to cry, how close had he just taken them to having a crash in the middle of nowhere, in the biggest snow storm the country has ever seen? He'd already lost the love of his life; he couldn't bare to imagine his children in pain.

Benny was screaming now. Kicking the chair in front of him, spit and snot falling down his bright red face.

Penny started to sing 'Oh, you pretty things,' stroking Benny's hand. By the time she'd run the chorus once, he had stopped crying. When she'd gone through it a second time. He was fast asleep.

'You're so good with him.' Jack said. Finally opening his eyes and getting over his shock.

'What are big sisters for?' She shrugged.

Jack put the car in to drive and set off down the road, this time at a snail's pace. His phone began to ping. *PING...PING...PING.*

'Oh, I must have got signal.' Jack said.

'Do you think we should call for help? At least let someone know we're here.' Penny said, highlighting the maturity levels beyond her years.

'No, it'll be fine.'

'What if we crash again and can't get the car started?'

'Penny. Honestly, we're fine. We can't be more than five miles from the lodge.'

Penny sat back in her seat unhappily.

They began descending down the other side of the mountain. The snow storm had let up, but was still coming down pretty heavy. The sudden drop in wind speed helped. That howling sound had started to become unsettling.

They reached a stretch of road that had forest on both sides, that stretched on as far as they could see. The solid white, snow filled road divided the forest into two. The steering began to get difficult. Jack persevered. It was three miles to the lodge now and he didn't want to stop if he could help it. The back of the car started drifting out, nearly sending them into the line of trees. 'Woah!' Jack yelled and frantically began turning the wheel the other way. He managed to correct it and got them heading straight.

'Dad, be careful!'

Jack stopped the car. 'I think we've got a flat.'

'What?'

Jack shook his head. He kept forgetting who he was talking to. 'A flat tyre sweet heart. It's making us slip and slide all over the road.'

'What are we going to do? Can we change it? Can we call someone to rescue us?'

'Hey! Calm down, ok? I'll get out and have a look. If I can't fix it, I'll call the owner of the lodge, they said they lived nearby in case we needed anything during our stay.'

Jack stepped out. As he opened the door, a blast of freezing cold air filled the car. Penny pulled away from it. Benny stirred in his sleep but thankfully didn't wake.

Penny watched Jack as he walked around the car, taking giant steps to get through the snow. She thought he looked like one of those astronauts they talked about in school who walked on the moon. He bent down and assessed the damage. When he came back, his face was all screwed up. She'd seen that face before, it wasn't a good news face. Jack opened the door and jumped back into the driver's seat. He shuddered; snowflakes fell from his coat.

Penny watched them melt into the fabric of the chair.

'God it's cold out there.' He said. His teeth chattered momentarily.

'Well?' Penny asked.

Jack shook his head. 'I can't fix it. I'll call the guy for a lift. We can sort it in the morning.' Jack picked up his phone, clicked about for a second and then put it to his ear. He pulled it away and looked at it confused, his brow all creased up to make his forehead full of horizontal lines.

'What dad? What is it?' Penny was sounding anxious to the point of a panic attack.

'It's ok sweetheart. I've just ran out of signal. I'll walk back up the road. It won't be far, then I'll make the call.

'Dad, what if the guy doesn't answer? What if you get stuck out there?' Another thought seemed to strike her. 'What if you don't come back? What if you leave us like mum did?'

She began to cry.

'Hey hey hey, I'm not going anywhere darling. I'll be five-ten minutes.'

She wiped her eyes and thought about it. Her breathing was heavy. She let out a long shuddering breath and it began to calm.

'Promise?'

Jack smiled and showed his teeth. 'I promise. And hey, think positive. What did mummy always say?'

"Positive thinking will get you through anything." They both said together.

'I'll keep the car running. Don't want it to get cold in here now do we? If you're hungry, there's a secret pack of chocolate biscuits in the glove box, but don't go eating them all.' He laughed and got out. He walked through the snow, walked up to her window and waved. She waved back and laughed when he drew a smiley face in the snow.

***

Penny sat in the car listening to the static of the radio and the steady breathing of Benny in the seat next to her. She was getting toasty with the heater on. She could deal with the heat but the sound of static was driving her crazy. She leant forward but the seatbelt stopped her from getting close enough to the radio in the front. She clicked the button to release it but nothing happened.

'Stupid thing...come...on...' She wrestled with it before giving up. She cursed the stupid old car and cursed her dad for not buying a better one. All of her friend's parents had the best cars, with big computer screens on the dashboard that told them which roads to take and where to go, and TVs in the headrests so they could watch films on long journey's. This one didn't even have cup holders. She sat back and accepted that she was going to have to listen to the static and deal with the heat until her dad came back. Thinking of her dad coming back, she turned to look out of the back window and couldn't see him. His footsteps that had been big black holes on a white sheet only moments before, were now almost re-filled with snow again.

The clock on the dash told her he'd been gone twenty minutes. Not five, not ten like he'd promised. She gave him the benefit of the doubt. An expression her mum had often used when she had done something wrong and dad had wanted to punish her by taking her TV privileges away. She would tell her mum that she didn't know it was real money she was cutting the queens face out of to stick on her barbie dolls. So mum said, 'Come on Jack, let's give Penny the benefit of the doubt.' For a while she thought she was actually going to be given something, and she didn't know if it was going to be a good thing or a bad thing. Eventually she understood that it meant she could basically get away with stuff if she didn't know it was bad

But, where was he? She looked again and still couldn't see him. Her heart started to pump faster and she felt that awful feeling in her stomach where she felt sick and full and dizzy and panicked, all at the same time. She looked at Benny and was relieved that he was still fast asleep. She couldn't cope if he started screaming again.

She looked out of her window and into the forest. The snow was falling, each flake seemed as big stones and as light as feathers. She took in a sharp breath when she saw something move amongst the trees. She wasn't sure what it was, but it was fast. Was it white? Grey? She tried to remember what she had seen but couldn't, it had happened too fast. But it was definitely something. Or was it? Her eyes began to hurt from trying to focus behind the wall of constantly falling snowflakes. She looked down at her hands until the dizziness drifted away and her heart calmed back down. She looked out towards the trees. Waiting for the thing to move again. She would get a better look at it this time, now she knows it's there. The trees were still. A branch broke deep in the forest, she heard it faintly. Snow fell from the tree tops in a great lump. She kept her focus, ignoring the steam forming on the window from her breath that she would usually draw in.

A gust of wind broke into the car and the door slammed shut. Penny turned and screamed, the noise scaring her to death.

'Shh honey. You'll wake Benny.' Jack shook his head to get the snow off his hood. His black coat had disappeared behind a thick layer of white.

'You were ages.' Penny said, her arms folded.

'Sorry sweetheart. The snow was really hard to walk through and I had to go up the hill to get a signal.' Jack took off his gloves and put his fingers on the vents that were pouring out hot air. 'God it's cold love.' He kept closing and extending his bright red fingers.

'Did you speak to the man?'

Jack kept his gaze set on his fingers.

'Dad?'

Penny pressed.

'Yeah...well, kinda.'

'What do you mean kinda?' Her voice held more than a hint of panic.

Jack took a deep breath and removed his woolly hat. Penny could see his face clearly now as he turned to face her. He was smiling but it didn't seem real, like it was a fake smile he was putting on to hide his true feelings. She knew because she'd seen that smile more than enough times over the past year.

'I left him a message. He might have been out or having his

dinner. Who knows, he could be really old and went to bed.' Jack noticed the fear grow in Penny's wide eyes so acted quickly to reassure her that everything was fine. 'The important thing to take away from this, is that we're safe, we're warm, the storm is passing and we're not that far from the lodge. If we have to, we can stay the night in the car, and have a nice leisurely walk in the snow to the cabin in the morning. It'll be fun. An unexpected adventure.

This seemed to work. Her breathing calmed instantly and the blood returned to her face.

'How will the man know where we are if he can't call you back?' She asked, never failing to surprise Jack with the maturity of her thought process. He bet there weren't many nine-year-olds who'd think of asking these questions.

'I told him exactly where we were, and told him we wouldn't be moving.' He smiled. A real one. 'Nothing bad's going to happen sweetheart. Trust me. Ok?'

Penny took three deep breaths. 'Ok.' She said looking back at the trees, thinking of the thing she had seen in there.

Then her tummy rumbled.

'Dad?'

'Yes, sweet heart?'

'Can I have a biscuit?'

***

It was pitch black outside. The storm had picked up again, the howling noise as the wind blew through the trees was keeping Penny from sleeping. Well, that and the fact that it was only nine o'clock and her bedtime on a weekend wasn't until nine thirty. When there was a break in the clouds, the full moon lit up the snow so brightly that it gave off a phosphorescent glow.

'Beautiful, isn't it?' Jack said, startling penny. He had been so quiet for so long she was sure that he'd gone to sleep.

'Yeah, it is. It looks like a postcard.' The road ahead was straight and long, black trees edged the pure white road, undisturbed by cars or foot prints. Human or otherwise.

Jack smiled to himself. 'Yeah. I guess it does.'

There was silence again for a short while. Until Penny finally broke it. 'Do you think mummy is watching over us?'

Jack shifted in his chair and sniffed. 'It doesn't really matter what I think sweety. What do you think?'

Penny thought about it. She hadn't given it much thought before. Whenever she thought about her mum, it was always about how much she missed her and wished she was still here. The idea of her looking down on them and being able to intervene at places in their life to keep them safe had never occurred to her. 'No. I don't think so.'

Jack turned around and looked at her surprised by what she said.

'What makes you say that?'

Penny slumped back in her seat and looked at her hands as she picked at the skin at the side of her finger nail. She shrugged.

'I don't know. Just a feeling.'

'If there is a God up there, he'll be looking after her, and I know, that she'll be looking down on you. She'd be so proud of the young girl you've become and how much you love and care for your little brother.' Jack reached his hand out and stroked Penny's leg. 'She loved you.'

'Then why didn't she try and fight it?' A tear rolled down Penny's cheek.

Jack's heart broke looking at Penny cry. She had kept it all in. He tried to remember a time when she had brought up Heather dying and couldn't. 'You know why darling. She made a decision. A hard decision, the hardest decision she would ever have to make. I know you're confused and angry about everything, and I know that's born from the sadness, but I promise you that you will understand. One day.' Penny said nothing. She rolled onto her side and tried to make a pillow with an old picnic blanket rolled up against the door.

***

Penny woke to Jack shaking her leg. 'I have to go to the toilet.' He said. 'I'll be two minutes. I didn't want you to panic if you woke up and saw I wasn't here.' He had his coat on but left his gloves and hat in the car. As he turned to get out, Penny grabbed his arm. She had been in a deep sleep and was still only half awake, but the need to grab him and tell him she loved him was overwhelming.

'I love you...you're doing a good job.' She said.

Jack laughed. 'I love you too sleepy head...and thanks... again. Go back to sleep.' He was about to step out when he stepped back in. 'Hey, I wish we could all sleep like Benny.'

Penny looked at her brother, he had his head tilted back, drool pouring down the side of his mouth, snoring away like he was the comfiest he'd ever been. Penny giggled and felt herself becoming more awake.

'Be back in two minutes sweet heart.'

Jack opened the door and shut it again quickly so they wouldn't lose too much heat. Penny shifted in her seat and pushed herself upright. She watched her dad go into the trees when her heart skipped in her chest.

What if there is something in the woods? What if hurts him and there's no way of getting help?

She watched with her face pressed against the window. If anything approached and worked its way towards the same area her dad was in, she'd scream and shout and bang on the glass to scare it off, or at least give her dad a warning so he could fight it off. She watched intently, convinced something was out there waiting, watching with the glowing yellow eyes of a predator. It wouldn't get past her and it wouldn't take her dad. Not if she could help it.

Her dad emerged from the trees, he staggered for a second and she let out a sharp cry, thinking he had been hurt. He had only slipped in the snow which gave her some blessed relief. As he made his way towards the car, he stopped and looked back in the direction they came from. He rubbed his eyes as if he couldn't believe what he was seeing. He walked in front of the car and out on to the road and began tentatively waving. Penny turned and looked out of the back window. Two small headlights were approaching from the distance. They were getting bigger and closer quicker than she thought they should be. Especially in this weather.

Jack stepped further out into the road and waved both hands above his head.

The car kept travelling towards them. It wasn't a car, not like theirs. Penny could see it was one of those big pick-up trucks with the big wheels that could drive on anything. She wasn't sure, but it didn't seem to be slowing down. She looked back at her dad and saw he was squinting, struggling with the wind blowing snow straight into his face. He used one hand to cover his face from the snow and the other one to wave, now frantically, in the air.

'Stop. Please stop.' Penny said quietly to herself, watching as the car approached. The car began drifting from side to side, not drastically, but enough to know that the driver didn't have full control going through such deep snow at that speed. She realised it before Jack did. The car wasn't going to stop. She looked back at her dad and saw he was still stood there, wiping snow from his eyes, he bent over and wiped his face, still trying to wave with one hand. 'Dad! It's not slowing down! It's not going to stop!'

Jack realised too late. He attempted to jump, more up then to the side, it wouldn't have mattered either way. The truck hit him and flung him up in the air. He flipped twice before hitting the ground. The truck skidded a further forty metres down the road, finally coming to a stop on an angle. Jack laid face down in the snow, not ten steps away from Penny's window. She wanted to scream but couldn't.

Had that really happened? Was it all a dream?

She looked from her motionless dad to the truck sat still down the road, it's engine rumbling idly as the driver, who Penny couldn't see from this far away, sat in the driver's seat, no doubt asking himself similar questions to the ones Penny had just asked herself.   The door of the truck opened. A man stepped out, a big man with a bald head. He walked into the light cast from the car's headlights. A trickle of blood began to drip down his face from a cut on his forehead. He staggered towards her, his hands swinging by his side. He slammed his hands on the bonnet. Then it felt real. Then she started screaming.

CHAPTER 2.

Penny screamed as loud as she could, hoping her dad would hear her cries and get up to save her. He didn't. The man looked at her through the windscreen and she back at him. The image of him was clear for only five seconds until the window filled with snow, then the wipers came to life and cleared it away, giving her five more seconds of unobscured sight.

When Penny stopped screaming, so she could catch her breath, she heard Benny screaming for the first time. He had woken up to the sound of gut wrenching, panic inducing screams that terrified him. Penny could only imagine his confusion, but thought she had a good idea on how scared he was.

The man made his way around the car to the driver's door, holding on to the car with both hands as he shimmied around. Penny instinctively tried to push herself away, kicking the chair with her feet to try and get closer to Benny. She manged to get so far before the belt stuck. 'Stop crying Benny. Stop crying.' She tried to tell him with tears of her own streaming down her cheeks.

The man opened the door and put his head inside. The car filled with cold air, Penny's long hair flapped in front of her face and into her gaping mouth. The man had a line of blood that ran down his nose and dripped into his moustache. He opened his mouth and let out a series of pants, like a dog. His breath stank of something Penny had smelt before; she didn't like it then and she doesn't like it now. It was the smell of beer, like what her dad drank when she went to bed. She had only smelt it when she woke up from a nightmare and he comforted her in the arm chair where he sat, with at least ten empty cans crushed by his feet.

'I didn't… didn't mean to.' The man slurred his words and let out one lonely sob. 'I didn't see you…tail lights…You've got no taillights.' His eyes were bouncing from side to side as he replayed the accident in his head. He snapped his head round and looked towards where Jack lay on the road. The brilliant white snow began to turn dark around him.

Penny held on to Benny who had stopped screaming and now just sobbed into his sister's arm. Holding it over his face.

The man looked back at the two children sat staring at him with fear filled faces. He dabbed the cut on his head, seeming to only notice the blood dripping from his nose for the first time. He looked at the blood on his fingers, and then looked back at the children. His eyes widened when something seemed to dawn on him. A great gust of wind rocked the car and filled it with freezing cold air that turned Penny's skin to goosebumps.

'Help him. Please, you have to help my dad.' Penny managed to say somehow. She felt as if she was out of her body, watching everything take place. If someone had told her to tell them her name, she doubted she would be able to.

'I'm sorry.' The man said. He looked at Penny and then at Benny. 'I'm so sorry. Please forgive me.' He crossed himself, like a vicar in church. He pulled his head out of the car and slammed the door shut.

'No.' Penny says, sliding herself over to the window. Benny grabbed her arm and screamed for her to stay with him.

The man put his face near the window, wiped away the snow next to the smiley face her dad had drawn earlier. 'I'm sorry.' He mouthed. He turned and waddled through the deep snow back to his truck.

'No! You can't leave him! You have to help us!' She screamed and hit the window as hard she could but it was no use. The man made it back to his truck. Snow spat up into the air as his big winter tyres spun until they caught a grip. The truck moved off into the distance, the red taillights getting further and further away until they disappeared completely.

***

Benny stopped crying. The car sat rumbling; the cold air the man had let in had been replaced with warm air from the car vents. Penny sat looking out of the window, watching as her dad slowly disappeared under the snow. The growing red circle around him had finally stopped. She wondered how much blood he'd lost. She knew there was only so much you could lose before you died, but she didn't know how much that was. It was one a.m. it had been over thirty minutes since the man left in his truck. She had cried for the most of that time, screamed for a part of it as well. She couldn't un-do the seatbelt. She didn't know what she would do if she did, all she knew was that she needed to get to her dad and see if he was ok. She couldn't drag him, but she could put the warm blanket around him. Try and roll him off of his face so he could breathe (if he was still breathing) but the seat belt was stuck hard. She thought she could wriggle out of it like she used to, but she was too big for that now, and the stupid booster seat that dad made her sit in made that impossible, 'a design feature to keep her safe', he had told her, now it could do the opposite.

She didn't know what to do. She was ten-years-old, in a situation she couldn't have dreamt up in a million years. Since her mum died, she had feared that her dad would leave her. The psychologist her school made her see for a short while afterwards, told her that was a natural way to feel after losing a parent. The fear of being left alone was common, that's why children who lose a parent grow-up that bit quicker than other children, because they need to know what needs to be done and how to do things. That way, if they are left alone, they'll be in a better position to survive. It was the brains natural survival technique. Penny didn't give it much thought when she said it, but now she realised, that's exactly what she had been doing. For the first time in her life, she closed her eyes and prayed. 'Please God, help us get out of this and let my dad live. You were cruel to take my mummy from me, if you are God, then please don't take my daddy too.' She wasn't sure if that was how people said their prayers, but it couldn't be too far wrong. You just ask him for what you want and most of the time, he won't answer, but sometimes, he will. Then she remembered the last bit you're supposed to say. She shut her eyes and closed her hands together.

'Amen.'

Benny started to cry again. 'Penn-ee.' he said between sobs. Penny looked at him. His bottom lip was protruding and his eyes glistened wet with tears. She shifted over as best she could, dragging the booster along the back seat with her and held his hand.

'Oh, you pretty things.' She started singing. Benny stopped crying and before he drifted back to sleep, he smiled. Penny smiled at how cute he looked. It made her feel happy, sad…a bit angry too. The psychiatrist had said that was normal, considering. When she knew Benny was fully asleep, she let go of his hand.

CHAPTER 3.

Three years ago.

Jack pulled his Ford into the driveway. Back then it still had that just off the forecourt glow, the door hinges didn't screech and the seatbelt buckles all clipped in and out like they should. He put the car in park and ran into the house, holding his phone in one hand and the car keys in another. 'Heather!' he shouted as he walked in the front door of their modest two up two down semi. He shouted again up the stairs and when there was no answer he walked into the sitting room. Penny, his then seven-year-old daughter, ran up to him with her arms outstretched.

'Daddee!' she screamed in delight. Jack bent and picked her up. Planted a kiss on her lips and swung her round to rest her on his hip. She was getting heavier everyday, but as he told Heather the night before, he'd carry that girl until his arms fell off his body.

Jack looked over at Heather, sat on the sofa smiling at him with a great big, beautiful grin and something clutched preciously in her hands.

'What is it? I thought something was wrong when you said to get home as soon as possible.' He was breathing heavily out of a panic that was still refusing to accept that everything was OK.

Heather stood and walked over toward him. She sat smiling and almost giggling with excitement. Penny giggled too and when Jack looked at her, she looked as though she was about to burst. Unable to hold back a smile, the palpable excitement in the room seemingly extremely infectious.

'What is it? Go on, tell me.'

'Jack... I'm -'

'I'm going to have a baby brother or sister!' Penny blurted out, unable to hold it in any longer.

'W-what?' Jack stuttered.

Heather put her arms around both of them and nodded. Her eyes filled with tears, then, as infectious as the excitement, so did Jack's.

'How? I mean... How?' Jack asked, shaking his head perplexed.

'It's a miracle Jack. Our prayers had been answered.' Heather said.

'But the doctor said it was impossible?'

'He said it was a one in a million chance. Not impossible.' Heather corrected. They all hugged, three was about to come four and in their own sense, complete.

Later that night, with Penny in bed, tucked in and fast asleep, Jack and Heather laid in their own bed with, the only light coming from the bedside table lamp. They talked about how far they'd come. Reminisced in amazement, working through all that they had been through to get where they are now. After Penny was born, they were desperate for another. The perfect ideal of having two children similar in age to grow up as friends and look out for one another, was a vision they both shared. They tried for nine months before deciding to consult a doctor. Heather was sent for the necessary scans and tests, while Jack was put in a room no bigger than a toilet cubicle, handed a magazine and a small plastic pot and told 'fill it up' by the smiling, young male receptionist. The tests came back, Jack's swimmers were good, not great, but only just falling behind the average for his age bracket. The problem was Heather. She had one working ovary, and even that one didn't want to do the job it had been designed for.

'You'll never conceive naturally. The fact you've already had a child is a miracle in itself.' The doctor had told them, sympathetically.

'What are our options?' Heather asked. Jack admired, as he always did, her strength and faith that things would work out. Always thinking of the positives. She didn't look panicked or upset, even though he knew she was. He on the other hand felt a dark cloud of sorrow flood over him. Thankfully Heather was able to ask all the questions he wanted to, but didn't have the strength to say out loud.

'Well,' said the doctor, stroking his chin thoughtfully, 'there is IVF. I've got some leaflets.' He reached into his drawer and gave them a leaflet each. 'The first round is free on the NHS. If that works, which, I'll be honest, is still a big *if*. Then you're good to go. If it doesn't... It can get rather expensive.'

'How expensive?' Heather asked. Knowing they had exactly zero in savings and Jack's job brought in an average wage.

The doctor screwed up his face in a grimace. 'I've seen families go bankrupt and penniless in their pursuit of having another child. Then the strain breaks up the family they had to begin with, ending in divorce and ugly, ugly scenes.'

Jack and Heather held hands tightly.

'My advice. If you want it. You have a wonderful family, and a beautiful little girl. Do the free round of IVF, by all means. But don't let it dominate your life. Enjoy what you have, it is more than a lot of people are blessed with.'

Heather nodded, swallowed away the lump that had formed in her throat and smiled through the tears at Jack who smiled back. 'Thank you doctor. You've been a great help.'

They held each other, neither one able to stop from smiling as they revisited the conversation with their doctor. 'We had got on with our lives after the first round of IVF failed, barely even spoke about it with each other. I didn't think it would ever happen.' Jack said, stroking Heather's flat belly that would soon be a bump big enough to think there were two babies in there.

'Yes, but we thought about it every day. Even if we didn't consciously think and wish for it, it was always there in the back of minds.' Heather put her hand on top of Jack's and smiled looking down at her stomach. 'I knew this day would come. Despite everything the doctors said. I knew we'd get the last piece needed to complete us.'

'I didn't.'

'I know. But that's ok. I prayed enough for the both us. Faith and positive thinking can get you through anything.'

Jack smiled and shook his head. 'You're amazing. You know that?'

Heather rested her head on Jack's. 'I do.'

CHAPTER 4.

Penny woke with a start. She checked Benny was still there and was relieved that he was. She put a hand over her heart, feeling it thump against her ribs, then looked out of the window for a fresh stab of reality. Her dad laid out there, barely visible now with all the snow that covered him. Bits of his black coat still visible, but she doubted anyone would see him if they didn't know he was there already. Benny was asleep, his nappy was bulging so much it was moulding around the buckle of his seat belt. She could smell it. Stale urine, exacerbated by the heat made her gag when she thought about it too much. She wound down her window using the twisty handle, just a crack, just enough to blow in some fresh air so she could catch her breath. She knew she'd have to change Benny's nappy sooner rather than later, but to do that she would have to un-do her seatbelt. She felt mounting pressure, she had to check on her dad, she had to look after Benny. What would she do if dad was dead? She couldn't look after Benny herself. They didn't even have any food. Her tummy rumbled at the thought.

Biscuits! She thought. She looked on to the passenger seat and there they were. Half a pack of chocolate covered biscuits where her dad had left them. The chocolate was melting, she could see it dripping through the plastic packaging on to the map. The chocolate collected on the edge of the wrapper, the drip getting bigger and bigger until it fell and splashed on to the map, soaking into the paper. It reminded her of the man's blood, dripping from his nose. She thought of his eyes, the look of guilt and fear he had right before he ran away. Leaving them to die in the snow. She hoped he would come back. He'd realise what he did was wrong and he'd come back. If not, then she hoped that he crashed on the way back to wherever it was he called home, and he was sat in a ditch, dead. She wiped an angry tear from her eye. She had cried too much. It was time for action and if she wasn't going to act then no one else would. She had two options. The way she saw it. She could either find a way out of this seat belt, or she could just sit there and wait for God knows how long until someone uses this road again. She wasn't one for sitting around. She had to step up and keep Benny safe. She grabbed the seat belt buckle with both hands, depressed the red lever that should release the lock and she pulled with all of her strength. The buckle came out enough that she could see the metal but not enough to come undone. Sweat was gathering on her forehead and falling in beads that soaked into her eye brows and stung her eyes. 'Come on!' She said through gritted teeth, pulling on the buckle until her arms began to shake and her face turned red. She felt it starting to budge, she was doing it, any minute now and it would come.

Something sounded outside that sent a freezing chill through her body and down her spine. It was a howl, something she heard on scary movies her dad let her watch when it was Halloween. The howl of a werewolf. She looked out the windscreen and saw the full moon sat above the snow filled road. The dark clouds seemed to form a ring around it, the glow that came from the moon seemed brighter than any light. The line of trees were lit up, they looked like they were standing guard at the side of the road, refusing to let anyone into the wood. She looked back to where she thought she saw something moving earlier when she heard the howl again. It came from behind her, to the side, in front, it was everywhere. The howl echoed in from all directions. Did Scotland have wolves? She didn't think so, but what else could it be? Were werewolves real? Dad had always told her they were make believe, like Dracula and Zombies. Maybe dads don't know everything?

Penny moved closer to Benny and held onto him tight. He opened one sleepy eye and let out a low cry of discomfort. 'Bum.' He said and started pulling on his swollen nappy.

'Shush Benny. Quiet.' Penny whispered.

'BUM! NAPPY!' He began to shout. The howls outside answered him, louder than they had been before.

'Oh my God Benny please be quiet. Ssshhhh.' She put her finger to his lips which only frustrated him more. He began screaming.

'Change my bum! Change my bum!' He screeched from the top of his lungs.

'Benny, shut the hell up!' She shouted, lunging across the car and putting her face into his. Benny stopped crying immediately, his eyes went wide with shock. Penny kept still and didn't say a word. Her eyes darted to the sides, looking out the windows. She thought she saw something, movement, a tree branch bouncing in the wind, its shadow stretching across the white floor.

The wolves had stopped howling. The moon was being swallowed up by dark clouds, bit by bit.

As Penny stood over Benny, she realised her shoulder felt different, like a weight had been lifted. A pressure had been released. When she looked, she saw the mark in her jumper where the seat belt had been.

CHAPTER 5.

Penny laid with head on Heather's belly. It was big and round now instead of flat and toned.

'Can you feel him honey?' They had found out it was a boy during their last scan. They wanted to know so they could plan how to decorate the nursery in the new house they'd just put a deposit down for.

'He's super wiggly.' Penny giggled. 'He keeps kicking my face!' They both laughed.

'Six months has just flown by. Hasn't it?' Jack said, coming in the living room. He wore a shirt that was spattered with baby blue paint.

'How's the decorating coming?' Heather asked, looking up from her belly to receive a kiss from Jack. She pulled a face. 'Your lips taste all sweaty.' She laughed.

'It's red hot up there!' He wiped his face with his shirt sleeve. 'All done. Ceiling, walls and woodwork. Finito.'

Heather clapped her hands together and laughed excitedly. 'Let me see!'

Penny jumped off the sofa and ran for the stairs first, eager to always be a part of it all, and be first in line for everything. Jack helped Heather up from the sofa when she winced and doubled over.

'What is it? What's wrong? Is it the baby?' Jack worried.

'It's my back. It's been killing me lately.'

'Do you need the hospital?'

She shook her head and took a few deep breaths. 'No, I'm ok. I just need a minute.' She paused and then went to stand. When she got as tall as she could, she winced again at the sharp pain in her back. 'Nope, I'm going to have to sit again.'

'Listen, maybe just put your feet up for a while. Ok?' Jack said, lowering Heather gently down to the sofa.

Heather nodded.

'I'll get you nice and comfy down here. I'll go upstairs, set the bedroom out so it's like a pregnant woman's paradise. There'll be flowers, chocolates, massage oil, hot water bottles, hot chocolate with whipped cream and marshmallows. And you can buy any Romantic comedy you want from the Sky box. Sound good?'

'Perfect.' She forced a smile. 'Jack?'

'Yes, sweet heart.' Jack began fluffing the pillows and putting them behind Heather as she leant back slowly.

'I don't like this.'

'Me neither sweetheart, it sucks.'

'No. I mean, something doesn't feel right. I think we should maybe go to the hospital.'

'If it carries on, then yes. I think you just need to rest. A nice hot bath and some bath salts might just work out those muscles for you.'

'Jack! I know my body. Something's not right.'

Jack only had to take one look in Heather's eyes to feel the same way. '

'On it.' Jack ran and got the car keys then went to the bottom of the stairs. 'Penny, we've got to nip out. Come down and get your shoes on.'

Penny came running down the stairs. 'Dad, the nursery looks amazing! I want a blue room too!'

'Maybe I can do yours after then.'

***

'Mr and Mrs Thompson,' The doctor started. An old man with short grey hair that grew only on the sides of his head. 'I've read through your notes and judging from your situation, you are understandably anxious. The fact you've fallen pregnant at all, is quite unbelievable.' 'So, do you think we should be concerned?' Heather asked. She was gripping Jack's hand tightly. Jack could see she the smile on her face was forced. For the first time in a long time, she looked to be having doubts, her positive thinking failing her. Penny sat in the corner watching an episode of Peppa Pig on Jack's phone.

The doctor leaned back in his chair and smiled, almost smugly. 'Mrs Thompson.'

'Heather. Call me Heather.' She interrupts.

The doctor nods. 'Heather, back pain is extremely common in pregnant women. Maybe you've forgotten because it's been so long since you were pregnant with Penny over there. Sometimes it can lead to something more painful, sciatica maybe, but in general...' He shrugged his shoulders and raised his open palmed hands, 'It's just the price you pay for being pregnant. So no, I don't think there's anything to worry about.'

Heather looked at Jack and raised her eyebrows. An unspoken expression that he knew to mean, 'Tag, you're in.'

Jack cleared his throat. 'Excuse me doctor, but, with all due respect. You haven't even examined my wife.'

'I understand, but back pain is back pain. If every pregnant woman who had back pain came in here, I wouldn't have time to see any body else.'

'Again, all due respect, my wife knows her body. She knows the difference between back pain and something else. If she tells me that she believes it's something that needs to be checked, then we're getting it checked.' Jack didn't raise his voice, but spoke clear and confidently. Heather liked that side of him. It was what made her fall in love with him all those years ago. That and his rugged good looks which enviously have only got better, she thinks, looking at him now.

'It's a waste of time.' The doctor, said, clasping his hands in front of his unhealthy swollen stomach. Looking down his nose in a way that looked to Heather as being condescending and down right patronizing.

Heather took a deep breath, put on her best smile, and said: 'Doctor. Will you please just make sure my baby is ok. That's all I ask.'

The doctor looked from Jack to heather, then to his watch. He put his pen down on the desk. 'Get up on the table.'

***

The scan of the baby was good. Strong heartbeat, two arms, two legs, healthy. No worry there. The doctor then looked at Heather, concerned when he saw the pain she was in and where the pain was radiating from.

'Mrs Thompson, excuse me, Heather. Can I ask, have you had anything else that has caused you concern?'

Heather turns out her bottom lip and shakes her head.

'Such as?'

'Blood in your urine? For example?'

Heather felt a jolt of panic go through her. 'Yes, but it only happened the once and the baby was moving round so much I didn't think I had to worry about him.'

The doctor scratched his stubble. Jack took notice of the change in his demeanour. Casual at first, like he was talking with friends in line at the grocery store, brushing off their concerns as though they were nothing, now Jack could see the other side of him. His professionalism came to the fore, cogs turning in his highly experienced doctor's brain.

'Turn around and lift up your shirt, if you please. If you would like a chaperone, I can call in one of the nurses?'

'No, it's fine.' Heather flashed a worried smile at Jack and saw Penny was yet to look up from the phone she was holding on her lap.

The doctor began to massage Heather's lower back. 'Tell me when you feel pain.' He said. He thumbed into her muscles. Rotating them in a clockwise motion. It all hurt, but Heather didn't feel that she could say that. Until he hit a small lump off to the right on the small of her back.

'Ow shit! There!' She cried.

The doctor let go and pulled down her shirt. He sat in his chair and pushed back so he glided across the floor to his desk. He began typing frantically, hitting the keys on the keyboard hard enough to push them through to the other side. With a final flurry he hit the return key and spun to face them. Heather sat back in her chair beside Jack, they leaned in towards each other subconsciously and gripped their hands in anticipation of some news they didn't think would be good news. The doctors face looked grave and drained of colour.

'I've put through an urgent appointment. You're going to require an MRI scan at the hospital. By the time you get there, they will have received it. Thankfully you live in a small town and the chances of the MRI being in full use all day is slim to none.'

Jack and Heather looked at each other confused.

'W-wait…an MRI? What for doctor?' Jack asked.

'I can't be sure until you've had the necessary tests.'

'But you've got an idea?' Heather added.

The doctor scratched at his stubble again. 'I'm probably wrong, you're young so I should be wrong but…You're showing signs for renal cell carcinoma.'

'What's that?' Jack asked.

Heather took in a heavy breath and her lip trembled. 'Cancer.'

***

The MRI was loud and terrifying. Heather hated having to do it without Jack by her side. Without the help of their own parents, (both sets died several years earlier) they had no one to take care of Penny. She was good, as always. She did as she was told and she sat in the waiting room. Thankfully the room was fully equipped with Sky tv and toys for all ages that kept her entertained enough that Jack could sit and run through every possible eventuality that they could have to face depending on the results of the scan.

'Will Mummy be ok?' Penny asked.

'She sure will sweet heart.' Jack said, sounding more positive than he felt.

The MRI done, they all got back in the car and headed home. They had just turned on to their street when Heather's phone rang. It was the hospital. They asked if they could come back in to go through the test results. Heather said 'Ok' and hung up.

'I thought they said the results wouldn't be for two weeks?' Jack said.

Heather shrugged.

***

Renal cell carcinoma. The doctor's hunch was right. Cancer of the kidney.

'How can this be? I'm thirty-six.'

The oncologist, a nice-looking man, middle aged with a comforting and friendly smile reached out and touched Heather's free hand. 'There is no rhyme or reason for these things. Cancer doesn't discriminate.'

Jack let out a choked sob and stood. He walked towards the window and covered his mouth. Heather kept herself together in a way that Jack could only admire.

'Ok. What's the plan?' Heather said. She cleared her throat and sat up straight. 'There must be a course of treatment, surgery, something?'

'There are yes, but each option, comes with…complications.' The doctor's eyes glanced down at her bump and then back to her eyes. Intentionally or not, Heather got the message. She stroked her bump and then felt Jack's hand close in on top of hers. He had composed himself and joined them once more.

'What do we do doctor, tell us what we need to do. Anything. You name it.'

The doctor leaned his neck and cracked out some of the tension he was feeling. 'The renal cell carcinoma isn't all we found. Kidney cancer can be hard to diagnose. There a few symptoms until the cancer is well established. The lump on your back the doctor felt, is the tumour. Cancer of the kidney is extremely aggressive. Judging from your scan…' He stopped and looked towards his computer where a black and white photo of the inside of Heather's body was set on the screen. 'We can see the cancer has spread to your lymph nodes, and your bladder.'

'Oh, dear God.' Jack felt a fresh wave of tears building. He put his arm around Heather and pulled her towards him, kissing the side of her head. She could feel his tears soak into her hair.

Heather felt numb, like she was in a nasty dream that she couldn't wake up from. She thanked God that they left Penny in the waiting room.

'I know this is a lot to take in. But if we are to stand any chance at all of beating this, we need to act fast. The way I see it, you have two options.'

Heather and Jack stared pleadingly at the doctor, hanging off his every word, waiting for him to tell them how he was going to make it all ok, that's what doctors did, isn't it? Make people better when they're sick?

'Option one: We operate, remove the cancerous kidney and find you a donor. Jack you can get tested if you choose to.'

'Of course, anything.'

'Then you'll start a course of radiotherapy and chemotherapy. This option, tragically I'm afraid, will mean losing the baby.'

Heather's lip began to quiver and she shook her head.

'Option two: We attack the cancer with the radiotherapy and chemotherapy, in the hope that will kill some of the cancer and halt the progression of the tumour's growth so that once the baby has been delivered, we can then perform the surgery.'

'Wait.' Heather held up her hand. 'Won't the Chemo and the radiation harm the baby?'

The doctor sighed; his face looked painful. 'Yes. And there is a chance that this option results in miscarriage.'

'No then.' Heather said defiantly. 'This is our baby; our miracle baby and I will not put it in danger.'

'Heather?' Jack looked at her with wide tear-filled eyes.

'No Jack. It's not up for discussion.'

'I have to interject. These are your only options if you are to stand a chance of beating this thing.'

The room was silent. The ticking that came from the clock on the wall seemed to get louder and louder, slower and slower, filling the void that hung between them.

'There is a third option.' Heather said. 'We wait until after the baby is born. Then we do the operation, do the Chemo and everything.'

'As I said, the cancer is aggressive.'

'But there is a chance that would work?' Heather held up a finger, interrupting the doctor.

'There is a chance. A very small, minute chance.' The doctor conceded.

'Heather, we need to talk about this.' Jack said, turning in his chair to face her.

She looked at him and put her forehead into his. 'We have to do this, for our son. He deserves to live. As hard as this test is going to be for us, I believe we can do it but I need you with me Jack. I need you to believe, to be positive every step of the way. Can you do that Jack?'

Jack nodded.

'Ok.' Heather let out a laugh through fresh tears.

'We'll wait until after the baby's born.'

The doctor pinched the bridge of his nose. 'You're sure?'

'Yes.' They both said.

'Ok then. We're going to have to deliver the baby early via c-section, how far along are you?' He began to check the notes on the computer.

'Twenty-six weeks.' Heather told him without missing a beat.

'Right. I think we deliver baby at thirty weeks and start treatment right away.'

'Thirty weeks is too early.'

'Under a controlled environment, with all the right equipment ready and prepared, thirty weeks is safe. Once upon a time, the little mite wouldn't have stood a chance, now babies at twenty-four weeks are surviving thanks to all the technology we have available.'

Heather shook her head. 'Thirty-four weeks.' She counter offered, as though she bargaining down at the local market.

'Thirty-two.' The doctor added reluctantly. 'But I'm putting my foot down on that Heather. You have a young family that's going to need you around.'

Heather smiled and held Jack's hand. 'We're going to be ok. It's all going to be ok. Think positive Jack.'

CHAPTER 6.

Penny felt around her waist, checking the belt really had gone. She looked at her seat and saw the metal buckle hanging where the belt had retracted back into its hole. She was free. Benny looked up at her, confused and nervous in case she shouted at him again. She didn't. She smiled.

'I'll be back.' She made her way to the door on her side. Locked. 'Child locks?' She grunted under her breath. Clambering over into the driver's seat, Benny made a whining noise and when she looked, she saw him reaching out for her. 'Two minutes Benny. I promise.' She said and thought of when her dad said those exact words, two minutes before he was run over by a drunk driver and ended up laying dead on the floor.

Not dead! She scalded herself. *Think Positive. You don't know that he's dead…not yet.*

She pulled the handle and the door opened. She was wary of the car losing heat so shut the door as quick as she could. She noticed for the first time that the wind had dropped to nothing. The snowflakes didn't so much fall as slowly drift to the ground, floating gracefully on the breathless air. She held out her hand and caught a few flakes before looking over at the snow mound that was her dad. She was stalling and she knew it. She walked over, her breathing grew heavy with panic, visible as clouds on the night air. Each step was difficult to take, as if her muscles were being controlled by something else that didn't want her to see what was under the snow. She fought against it, thinking only positive thoughts as she took each physically draining step, blocking out the bad thoughts, the thoughts that told her this was a lost cause, he was as dead as mum was and she was alone. It was up to her to make it through the night until somebody came to save them. Her foot stood on something uneven. She had reached the mound without realising it, her eyes had gone snow blind. She got on her knees, urgency now taking over her, she began to dig. She uncovered what she had stood on, her dad's hand. She moved up and dug faster, throwing snow out behind her until his face was revealed. His eyes were closed, she didn't know if that was a good or a bad sign. She felt his cheek with her hand. It was cold as ice. She tried to feel his neck for a pulse but didn't know what she was feeling for, she'd just seen it on TV.

'Dad.' She said, shaking him. His face didn't change. She began scraping all of the snow from him. His coat had kept his body dry, but his jeans were soaked through.

'Dad! Please wake up!' She said, shaking him madly this time. When she finished shaking him, he rolled on to his back. She could see a great gash down one side of his face full of dark clotted blood. His eye lids popped open and he stared blankly up at the night sky. Snow flakes continued to float down. Some melted on his cheeks, some landed in his mouth, on his eye ball. Only a couple melted until it started to settle. Her dad made no move to wipe his eye or clear his throat of the snow. He was dead. Penny began to cry. She fell onto her dad's cold, lifeless body and wept.

'You did a great job dad. You were the best.' She said and kissed his lips. They were cold and dry despite the melting snow.

The snow around her started to grow brighter, at first, she thought headlights were coming her way and she was going to share the same fate as her dad, but when she turned around, she saw it was just the moon breaking out from behind the clouds to illuminate the small part of the world Penny found herself trapped in.

She needed to move him. She accepted that. If someone did come, she didn't want them to run him over and make more of a mess of him than he already was. She knew he wouldn't feel it, but that didn't matter. He was still her dad.

Benny was shouting from the car. First things first. She thought. She had to change his nappy, get him clean and comfortable and maybe he'd sleep until morning. That would leave her some time free to drag her dad to the side of the road before curling up on the back seat of the car and trying to sleep. She stood and wiped her eyes free of tears. The feeling to cry was always there, waiting at the back of her throat wanting to burst out in screams and sobs but she had work to do. She opened the boot; it was heavy but once she got it halfway it went the rest of the way on its own.

She grabbed the nappy bag and reached up to shut the boot again. Conscious of the car filling with cold air the entire time she had it open. It was out of reach. She dropped the nappy bag to the floor and climbed in the boot. She stood, balancing herself with one foot on the rim and one in between the two suitcases. She reached up and got a hold of the boot handle. She pulled it down, which was hard in the position she was in, the boot didn't seem to want to. She finally managed to bring it down low enough that she could step out on to the floor and still keep hold of the handle, once with feet firmly planted, she was able to generate enough force (on the third attempt) to get the mechanism to clip and keep it shut. She grabbed the nappy bag, wiped it free from snow and got back in the car. The wolves began howling again. The howls sounded closer than before, so Penny hit the button that locked all of the car doors. Just in case Scottish wolves have figured out the complexities of a car door handle. You never know. Her fingers were swollen and red, they stung every time she touched something, as if everything she touched was made of needles. She sat with her hands on the vents, warming them through. Which hurt at first but soon felt nice and soothing. The radio crackled. A faint sound came through the static. It was the familiar voice of David Bowie, the radio was playing 'Oh, you pretty things again.' Penny knew that most radio stations played the same set of songs every 4-6 hours, but something about that song, being played throughout the day mad her think about the conversation she had with her dad when they saw the statue called 'The Angel of the north.' She wondered if the song playing through the radio, was a sign. That mum was watching over her and Benny, their very own guardian angel that would guide them through the danger and keep them from harm. Penny hoped that was true.

CHAPTER 7.

Penny could see after the hospital appointment that things weren't ok. Despite the smiling faces that looked down at her from both of her parents and the doctor. She was given a sticker for being a good girl and a lolly-pop for the ride home. Over the next six weeks, Penny noticed her mum hurting more, everything taking more effort and her back pain would keep her in bed for days sometimes.

'What's wrong with mummy?' Penny asked her dad when she was helping him put the shopping away in the kitchen cupboards.

Jack paused, a bag of pasta in his hand half in and half out of the cupboard he was putting it into. 'Listen sweety.' He said, coming back to life. 'Your mum has…well, she has bad disease inside of her.'

'Can't the doctor fix her?'

'They can, and they will, but they can't until they get the baby out. That's why your little brother will be born tomorrow, a whole two months early!' Jack was smiling but Penny wasn't buying it.

'They couldn't fix her before the baby came?'

'Well, they could have. But mum…but *we* thought it would be safer for your little brother to wait.' Jack noticed the worried look on Penny's face. He knelt down and cupped her chin in his hand. 'Everything's going to be ok sweetie. I promise.'

***

'Meet your brand new, baby brother.' Penny walked over to the incubator that was kept in a small dimly lit room. There were four incubators in total. One for every corner of the room, with a family surrounding each one. Penny walked up and pressed her head against the plastic wall of the incubator and looked in.

'He's so small.' She said.

'That's because of how early he was.' Jack said, bending down so his face was level with hers as they both looked at the baby. 'The doctor's say he's perfectly healthy. Just a bit small so he'll have to stay in this for a couple of weeks.'

Penny chewed her lip then turned to look at her dad.

'Where's mummy?'

Mummy's fine sweet heart. She's just having a talk with the doctor and then she'll be joining us.' Just then the doors swung open and in came Heather, she was sat in a wheel chair being pushed by an extremely happy black woman with short hair.

'Is this your gorgeous family Heather? My goodness. How beautiful they are.'

'Thanks.' Jack said and smiled.

'I meant the children, funny man.'

'Yes, they're my pretty things. Thank you, Julie.' Heather said, tapping Julie on the hand.

'No problem, Heather. You get better now, and enjoy those wonderful kiddies.'

Heather wheeled herself around to the other side of the incubator and gave Penny a huge hug. Penny wrapped her arms around her mum like she hadn't seen her in forever.

'I was worried.' Penny whispered.

'You don't have to worry. I'm fine. So is Benjamin.'

***

It was six weeks later when Benjamin was allowed home. Jack had kept on top of the place, as well as working (reduced hours to be able to do the school pickups) and taking care of Penny. The doctors wasted no time in introducing the chemotherapy. The tumour on her kidney and bladder had grown. They said the chances of them reducing to a small enough size to operate were sadly, extremely low. 'It'll be all right. I believe. We believe.' Heather said to the doctor. It wasn't just Jack that admired her strength. It was every doctor, nurse and fellow chemo recipient that admired her. She sat there, smiling the entire time it took for the poison to drain from the bag and into her veins so it could attack and kill the cells in her body, and hopefully get most of the cancerous ones with them. They hadn't kept it from Penny, but neither had they told her the extent of what was happening. Penny however, was an extremely perceptive young girl who could see what was happening. She heard the faint whispers at night. She saw the toilet bowl splattered in chunks of puke that had been missed when cleaning. She knew her mum's illness was far worse than what they were making it out to be.

The weeks turned into months and the months turned into a full year.

Penny was sat watching cartoons, Benjamin laid in his rocker next to her. Watching her more than the TV. If Benjamin became upset, as babies are wont to do, Penny would rock him and sing to him. Wheels on the bus was one of his favourites.

Heather came in, her hair was thinner, in some places there were massive bald spots where her hair should be. Penny had noticed but didn't say anything. Her mum had always loved her hair, she thought it might upset her if she pointed it out. Heather walked over towards them smiling. Her face thin and gaunt, her eyes looked as though they were set back in deep black sockets. The smile faded and Heather stumbled. She shot her hand out to the TV unit to steady herself. She missed but managed to stagger over to the sofa which broke her fall. Jack came running in when he heard the cries from Benjamin and the small shout from Heather.

'What happened?'

'I just…felt a bit light headed. That's all.'

Jack ran a hand through his hair. 'You need to be in bed.'

'I want to sit with my children.'

'Heather. You need rest.'

'Ok.' Heather sat herself up, her muscles aching, she struggled for breath. 'Take me to my chair.'

***

In Penny and Benjamin's bedroom, was Penny's bed, a small cot for Benjamin and a big comfy armchair they had bought for the night feeds. Jack helped Heather into it, then went downstairs to grab Benjamin. He placed the baby in her arms. Penny stood there silently, gripping Jack's hand.

'Come on.' Heather beckoned Penny forward and patted her free thigh.

Penny looked up at Jack. He nodded and Penny climbed up on to Heather's knee. Heather wrapped one arm around Penny and the other cradled Ben.

Penny snuggled in to her mum and for some reason, she felt like crying. She realised it had been so long since she had done this. Something she used to do a lot. They'd sit and watch Disney films on the sofa, with hot cocoa and chocolate bars. They hadn't done that for a long time. Her mum felt different then she had done before. Penny could feel every lump and bump of her mum's bones. She was so thin now. And weak.

Jack looked at them all and wiped his eyes. Heather smiled and mouthed. *Go put your feet up.* Jack mouthed back *you sure?* To which Heather nodded. Jack left the room so it was just Heather and her children. She looked down at both of them. One so small and one so big. Both still her babies.

'Oh, you pretty things.' She sang the whole song through until Benjamin was fast asleep.

'I love you mummy.' Penny said.

'I love you too.'

***

When Jack came back up stairs Penny, Benjamin and Heather were all fast asleep in the chair. He leant down to pick Benjamin up to put him in his cot when a quiet voice whispered to him.

'Leave him.' He looked up and saw Heather.

'You can't sleep here all night. You need your rest.' Heather shook her head lightly. 'Jack. My love. Rest isn't going to help. We both know I'm not going to win this.'

'What?' Jack said, his voice cracked slightly.

'The tumours aren't shrinking. They can't operate and my first round of chemo is almost over.'

'C'mon now. Where's the positive thinking? You can beat this. If anyone can, it's you. I won't accept it, we can do another round, one more blast. You have to fight.'

'I'm tired Jack. I have no fight left in me. Everything hurts. My whole-body screams at me, everything I touch feels like razor blades. I've already told the doctor's no to anymore treatment. I don't want the side effects to take over my last few months with my children.'

Jack rubbed Heather's leg and tried to hold back his sobs. 'I can't do this without you.'

Heather brushed a tear from his eye with her thumb and held his face. 'You can. You're the greatest father our children could have asked for. I am so proud of you for being so strong and believing with me. If not for that, I don't think I would have got another year under my belt. A whole extra year of watching our children grow up. Watch you being superman. We have to face that the cancer is winning.'

Jack shook his head. He held Heather's hand and kissed it.

'Nights like this. Going to sleep whilst holding both of my babies is all I want.'

'You're so brave.' Jack stroked Heather's face and pushed back her thin hair from her eyes. 'And so beautiful.'

They kissed and held each other, sobbing quietly. Penny kept her eyes closed, not wanting them to know she was awake. A single tear rolled from her eye before she forced herself to sleep.

CHAPTER 8

'There you go Benny.' All fresh. She buttoned up Benny's trousers and put him back in his car seat. Buckled him in tight so he didn't fall out of it when he fell asleep. It was the first nappy change she had ever done, apart from when Benny was still tiny and mum was still around. That was a long time ago now though. Or so it felt to Penny. She thought it funny how time can seem to be both so long ago and yet feel like yesterday.

Benny smiled again and that made her happy. A smiling Benny was a happy Benny, and that was something good. If he was happy that meant he didn't know what was happening outside.

That was better.

She covered Benny up with the blanket and sang 'Oh, you pretty things' until his eyelids grew heavy and he let out a tiny snore where he whistled at every breath in. She kissed his forehead and looked out to her dad lying on the ground. Her fingers had warmed through and were now back to their proper peachy flesh colour instead of bright red. She didn't want to go outside again and face the cold. In truth, what she really didn't want to face was her dad. She hated seeing his eyes, open and blank. He looked like he was just sleeping at first, but when his eyes opened, she realised that he wasn't there anymore. Which sounded weird as she ran these thoughts through her head but that's how it was. Mum's eyes were closed when she saw her. She wished dad had kept his eyes closed. It might have made it easier to go out and face him. The wolves let out one final howl, now so loud she was sure they had reached the car. Did wolves smell blood like sharks? Is that why they were howling? A celebration that they could smell food and they were going to feast? The thought made her angry and determined. She jumped in to the front seat and left the car. She ran over to her dad and grabbed his foot. He was wearing great big walking boots that were thankfully tied tight through all the small metal loops the laces passed through. She pulled as hard as she could. She couldn't budge him. She bent his knee and then ran two paces, hoping the speed mixed with her strength would help him along the snow. It didn't. 'Please! Come on!' She shouted and tried again. Grabbing his boot with both hands and pushing back with her legs. If she let go now, she would fall flat on her back and she wouldn't stand a chance to save herself. The wolves howled again. Her hand slipped and she fell into the snow. She lifted her head and looked around her. The trees were black and dark with shadows. Her eyes played tricks on her, seeing things that weren't there. Monsters, snakes, wolves; anything and everything scary she had ever seen was coming out of those shadows, and they were looking at her.

'Get to the car.' She whispered to herself. But her arms and legs wouldn't move. She was frozen stiff. Her muscles didn't want to do anything. Fear had gripped her hard and it wouldn't let go. Benny began to cry, she looked up and saw his sad face with the protruding bottom lip. Somehow, that gave her a shot of whatever chemical it was she needed to shake her muscles free of what gripped them. She ran to the car, the wolves' howls turned to barks. The sound of paws pounding on compacted snow got louder and louder. She ran to the car, her heart pounding in her chest, she could feel it thumping in her ears. She began to cry when she reached the car. Imagining what she would see if she turned around right then. A pack of ravenous wolves sprinting towards her, white teeth sat in snarling black lips, dripping with blood from the last dead thing they called dinner. Closing in on her, their feet pounding the snow-covered floor.

'Come on!' She screamed and opened the car door. She jumped in and slammed it closed behind her. She expected a thud on the car door, the window to smash from the force of the wolves' head butts. She cowered into a small ball. The barks and howls were so loud, they were right outside the car. She opened one eye and they stopped.

Had she imagined the whole thing? Why would they stop when they were so close to getting her?

She looked at Benny and saw he was looking out the window.
'What is it, Benny?' She whispered.
Benny looked at her and smiled.
'What's out there, Benny? What can you see?'

He clapped his hands together. 'Doggy.'

Slowly, Penny lifted her head and looked out of the window. Circling her dad's body, was a wolf. Its head was huge, and it had great big yellow eyes that shone in the moonlight. Its grey fur was long and shaggy. It looked and sniffed at Jack's body. Waiting to see if it would suddenly jump back to life. When the wolf knew Jack was dead, it began biting.

'NO!' Penny screamed. She hit the window. The wolf looked up at her, regarded her with nothing more than passing intrigue, and returned back to her meal. The wolf took a large bite on Jack's hand. Ragging and shaking to pry the fingers away from the hand. The wolf fell back. Penny saw Jack's hand was left with just a thumb and a pinky finger.

'Leave him alone!' Penny screamed, hitting the window harder this time.

Benny started crying and kicking his legs.

'Leave. Him. Alone!' Penny looked around the car for a weapon. There was nothing. Even if she did find something, she wouldn't have been able to wield it with any great power. But she had to do something. That was her dad out there.

She saw on the passenger seat the pack of chocolate biscuits. She grabbed them and opened the car door. The wolf looked up from its feast and let out a low warning growl.

Penny walked towards it slowly with her arms stretched out un threateningly.

'I'm not going to hurt you.' Penny said. The wolf kept its gaze on her, then took a step to the side to face her head on.

Penny gulped down her fear and carried on. 'Here boy.' She said, her voice shaking.

Every time Penny stepped forward, the wolf stepped closer.

The wolf growled, the distance between them only a couple of metres. 'Here boy, fetch.' Penny threw the biscuits into the woods and to her surprise, and relief, the wolf went in after them. She looked at where the wolf had entered the forest and saw not one, but three sets of yellow eyes staring back at her. There were more of them. All looking at her, their eyes glowing in the darkness; watching her every move. Slowly, keeping a watchful eye on the wolves watching her, Penny took a step back. Then another. Steadily, she picked up the pace, walking backwards towards the car. The wolves' eyes came forward, surrounded in darkness the eyes looked like they were floating in the air. Penny afforded herself a glance over her shoulder and saw the car was only a few steps away. She was close enough to make a dash for it. She turned and sprinted the last few strides. A bark and a snarl echoed loudly behind her. She heard the thud of paws as the beast landed in the snow and chased after her, fresh living prey must taste better than dead, she thought sickly.

She grabbed the door handle and swung it open. She dived inside, landing in the driver's seat. She reached for the handle to close it and she saw the wolf closing in. Its huge teeth were dripping with blood, its eyes looked less yellow now but full of a ferocious hunger as it galloped towards her. Penny let out a terrified scream. The door seemed heavy, for a split second she thought it was caught on something, but it was the fear making her weak. The wolf closed the gap until it was close enough that she could smell its rank breath.

'Leave me alone!' She screamed and found the strength to shut the door. The wolf slammed into the side of the car with such force that it left a huge dent in the metal.

Penny scurried across to the passenger seat, pushing herself against the door, getting as far from the window where the wolf stood snarling at her, licking its lips at the meal coming its way. Benny was staring at the wolf too; he was scared but he wasn't crying. Which Penny thought was odd because it didn't take much for Benny to start crying. He would cry over anything. She flashed a smile at him.

'It's going to be ok Benny. The doggy won't hurt us.'

Benny nodded.

The wolf had his paws up on the window, its claws were dragging against the glass, piercing the plastic window seal and dragging it off in strips. After five minutes, it grew bored. It gave Penny one last look and dropped its paws to the floor. It went back into the woods, back to the two sets of yellow eyes that waited patiently for it to return, and sat there, waiting.

Penny was relieved but confused. Why didn't the wolf go back for her dad? It had a meal right there and yet it went back into the woods. Then she realised. It was waiting for her. A live meal.

***

Penny kept her eyes gripped on the wolves in the forest for an hour. It was past two a.m., the latest she'd ever stayed awake until. Then her eyes started to grow heavy and she drifted in a half-asleep, half-awake daze. She kept having a sudden feeling that she was falling that snapped her to full alertness, she would check around, check Benny who was fast on, then she'd close her eyes again.

The radio crackled and she expected 'Oh, you pretty things' to play. Expected or hoped, either way, she had cemented the idea that whenever that song played on the radio, it was another sign from her mum, letting her know that everything would be ok. Someone would come and find them and take them somewhere safe. The man who owned the lodge they were driving to would pick up the message her dad left and come out to see them. But it wasn't David Bowie she heard on the radio. It was a man's voice, a new readers voice who was giving a round-up report of the day's events for those unlucky enough to be driving this late at night, long haul truckers or night shift workers, or children whose dad had been run over in the road like a dog and were now stuck in a car surrounded by blood thirsty wolves.

The voice was crackly at first, then a gust of wind must have pushed the signal just right because then the mans voice came through with perfect clarity.

'Police gave a statement today regarding the nine-year-old girl found in the Scottish Loch Lomond National Park in the early hours of this morning. The suspect is said to be driving a four-by-four vehicle. They are certain this man is responsible for two similar murders that shocked the country earlier this year, as well as the still missing Clare Halliday. Police have warned the public to be extra vigilant; make sure all your windows and doors are locked. This man is extremely dangerous, if you see anything phone this number.' The news caster began to crackle again. He could be heard giving out a phone number where people could phone up with any information, followed by an interview with the deceased girl's family, in a desperate plea for the man responsible to come forward, and to not hurt anyone else. Penny slips into a deep, dreamless sleep.

CHAPTER 9.

Penny woke up shivering. The tip of her nose was stone cold and she could see her breath floating into the air like smoke. She sat up; the back of her head hurt from leaning against the hard plastic of the interior door. 'What the hell?' She says, looking around the car for clues. Benny is still fast on although she can see his breath as he snores quietly in his chair, his head dropped low with his chin on his chest. She grabbed the blanket and put it on his lap, tucking it in at the sides.

She began rubbing the heat back into her arms, the more awake she became the more she realised how cold it was. Her teeth began chattering together, she put her tongue in between them to stop the rattling noise it made in her skull. Holding herself, trying to get warmer, she looked around for another blanket. She's sure she remembered seeing another one. Then she remembers. It's in the boot. She clambered into the back seat to see if she could reach into the boot from there. She can't. There's a small crack behind the back seats where she can see into the boot, but even Benny wouldn't be able to get his hand through there. She turns and flopped into the seat, holding her arms around her chest. The cold had seeped into her bones, it felt like she was being frozen from the inside out. She moved back to the driver's seat. The clock on the dash said 3:30 a.m. Looking at the dials behind the steering wheel, she could see the petrol gauge had gone past nothing. The electrics still worked, for now, but they won't last much longer without the engine going, she thinks.

The snow was still falling heavily. The heat of the running engine had kept it from settling on the car, but now it was six inches thick. They were being cocooned in snow. She remembered that some people in the world live in igloos, and they survive just fine. The car was just turning into one giant igloo. She shook her head. She didn't want to be in an igloo, and if the car came completely covered in snow, they'd be harder to find. Someone might just drive right past or, worse still, drive right into them. The window was caked in snow, impossible to see out of. She needed to see if the wolves had given up and gone on to somewhere else in search of food. She didn't dare step outside so she began slowly winding down the window. The snow stayed where it was even though the window was rolling down. Normally this would fascinate her. Now she doesn't pay it much attention. She closed her eyes and whispered a small prayer, asking for the wolves to be gone so she can clear off the car, and maybe, this just coming to her, be able to find dad's phone from his pocket and try and call 999. 'Amen.' She pushes at the snow with her hand and the whole screen of compacted snow collapses.

She falls back, screaming in terror when she sees the wolfs face peering in through the window. The wolf is standing so close to the car, a bit of the falling snow lands on its shiny black nose. The wolf snaps its huge jaws through the window. Instinctively, Penny kicks out at it, wildly thrusting her feet at the wolf, trying to hurt it enough to make it fall out of the window. She makes a connection two or three times but the wolf keeps snapping, trying to catch one of those feet in its jaws. She notices the fresh redness of its muzzle and thinks that it did get bored of waiting. It feasted on her dad, but it still wanted more.

Penny is screaming and kicking, Benny lifts his head, but can't open his eyes, his head falls back to his chest. Penny is glad, she doesn't want him to see what's about to happen. He might have a memory of it, and it will haunt him forever. He'll have to see a psychiatrist who'll give him tips on how to deal with the feelings he can't understand or process. She doesn't want that for him. Their mum died for him, and now it was Penny's job to look after him and keep him safe. She remembers telling her dad that he was 'doing a good job' it was the last thing she said to him before he died. She hopes he knew that she meant it.

The wolf howled and snapped at her foot again, its teeth pierced her boot but missed her toes.

She meant every word. He did the best for them that he could and she loved him for it. He did a great job and if he was here now, if he hadn't been hit by that stupid drunk driver, he would have kept them safe and kept them smiling.

Penny was growing tired, her thighs burned and ached from

trying to keep the wolf at bay, she wasn't sure she could go on much longer. She started to cry, she was crying for the loss of her mum, the loss of her dad, the idea of Benny growing up with no family around him. She was crying most of all because she was accepting defeat. She couldn't keep her legs up any more. She couldn't keep fighting.

CHAPTER 10.

The hospice that the nice chemotherapy nurse recommended was as lovely as she had said it would be. It had a nice garden outside that some patients could be wheeled out to enjoy. The flowers in the summer were supposed to be wonderfully bright and vibrant. It was late Autumn when Heather was admitted, so the flowers had started to wilt and the green of the trees had started to turn brown and fall from their branches. Penny hated the long walk down the corridor when she went to visit. Which was every day. Her dad told her she didn't have to come every day; he and Heather would understand if she would rather go to a friend's house for a few hours.

'It's a lot for someone your age to take in and deal with.' He'd say.

And every time, she'd respond with: 'She's my mum. Of course, I want to see her.'

The whole length of the corridor was painted a brilliant bright white, which made it feel as though it were miles long. It didn't have a single mark or blemish on it. The carpets were fluffy and cleaned daily, the toilets smelled of fresh flowers and apricots. Jack had told Penny that this was the place where people came for a comfortable ending. She wondered if the effort the nurses went to with the air fresheners was to cover the smell of death. This dark way of thinking was a far cry from what she used to think about. But since Benjamin (who had now become affectionately known as Benny) was born, the darkness in Penny's mind had grown, slowly taking over all of her thoughts. Death was a concept so far from her understanding a year ago, something that she shouldn't have to deal with for many years, now it was all she could think about. It was hard to think of anything else, when looking at her mum.

***

Heather laid in a single bed with a soft padded headboard. It was a soft pink colour that matched all the other furniture in the room and the bed spread. A series of monitors sat by her bedside and a bag of fluid was plugged into her arm to keep her hydrated. She didn't eat much, so the nutrients the bag of fluid provided her were essential. The wall was covered in pretty wallpaper that depicted a spring scene; bees gathering nectar from freshly bloomed flowers and baby birds hatching from their eggs in perfectly circular nests. The image repeated itself all the way along the wall.

Penny and Jack walked in and Benny slept in his pushchair. Penny gripped her dad's hand as tight as she could and looked down at her feet as they walked towards the bed. As desperate as she was to see her mum, Penny struggled to bring herself to look straight at her. Her mum had always been smiley and positive. Her smile was infectious, something about the way her cheeks pushed up to make it look as though they were extra chubby made it impossible to hold back a smile of your own when looking at her. She was always full of energy, willing to play any board game, get down on the floor and help Penny arrange her Barbies and get them dressed in different outfits for different occasions. That was the way Penny promised to remember her. Not the way she sees her now. Thin and pale, barely able to curl her lips into a smile. Her cheeks as sunken as her dark, black circled eyes. Her teeth were turning a grim shade of yellow. Her long flowing hair that had been taken by the chemotherapy had made a feeble attempt to grow back but only managed to appear in whisps and patches. Penny was amazed that the doctors managed to get a needle in to her arm without it coming out of the other side they were that thin.

'Hey guys.' Heather said weakly.

'Hello darling, I brought some visitors to see you.' Jack said, ushering Penny forward with his hand placed in the middle of her back.

Penny moved forward and sat in the arm chair by the side of the bed.

'It's so nice to…to…' Heather started to talk but her strength left her and she closed her eyes. Penny looked at

Jack who looked a mixture of worried and heart broken. Heather pinged her eyes back open. 'Sorry…so tired.' She smacked her dry lips together, Jack hurried to respond to her cue and grabbed her a cup of water with a straw to suck on.

'Thank you.' She said and lifted her arm to touch his face which looked as though it took everything she had.

Jack looked at the machine monitoring her heart rate and blood pressure, his head dropped slightly when he saw how low the numbers were. She was shutting down and he knew it.

The nurse came in with a clipboard. She had a bright face full of colour. She beamed a great smile that showed off her beautifully white teeth at Penny. Penny wished her mum still had that smile. She thought that it wasn't fair other people got to carry on when her mum didn't. 'Mr. Thompson. Can I have a word?' The nurse said to Jack.

'Yes, of course.' He looked at Penny and pointed towards Benny. *Will you watch him?* Is what that meant. Penny nodded in acknowledgment. She was getting used to watching Benny when her dad had to do something.

Penny sat in the chair, her feet were able to touch the ground now and it made her think that part of her childhood and gone. A year ago, she would have been swinging her feet, maybe while humming a tune or watching Peppa Pig on her dad's phone, now she just sat with her hands in her lap and her feet still on the floor. She checked in on Benny while her mum dosed in and out of consciousness. Benny was asleep. He would never remember this. His only knowledge of the mother he and Penny shared would be the photos. The memories of all the good times when she had all of her hair and she was strong enough to lift Penny up and carry her around all day. She felt jealous. She wished she wouldn't remember this, but she would, and she'd carry around the image of her mum laid in bed dying whilst she sat with her feet on the ground remembering her childhood that was dead and gone. Despite how hard she would try and force herself to forget. She would remember.

Jack comes back into the room. The nurse gave a sympathetic look through the door before turning and walking away down the hallway. Jack's eyes were swollen and red, he was smiling the fake smile he put on to hide how he was really feeling. He rubbed Penny's hair and then gave her a big hug. He tried to talk but his voice wouldn't come out. He stood and turned to Heather, he held her gently so as not to hurt her, she bruised so easily now. He whispered: 'I love you. So Much.' And kissed her on the cheek. Heather didn't respond. Her chest rose slowly, then deflated back down. 'We'll always remember you.'

Penny knows why her dad can't speak. They've been waiting for this day and it was finally here. As much as her dad prepared her for it, she never knew how she would feel until it came. The day they would have to say goodbye and never see her mum again. Now that day was here, she felt broken.

CHAPTER 11.

Penny couldn't keep her legs up any longer, the wolf was wearing her down, her left boot had been torn to shreds, the wind began to pick up and sent in icy blasts that stung her face. The wolf snarled and spat as she kicked at it. It stopped biting and pulled back. Penny kept her legs in the air protectively, they were shaking so uncontrollably she had to drop them. The wolf leaned in again, its bared teeth looking like a grin, and moved closer to her. She was exhausted, she couldn't put her legs up again to ward it off even if she wanted to. She'd given up. She thought then about how tired her mum must have been, and how scared she must have been without ever showing it. Mum did that for them, so Benny could live and she could have a brother. 'I'm sorry mum. I couldn't be as strong as you.' She whispered, letting go of all the anger and confusion she felt about her mum.

The wolf opened its jaws, a string of red saliva stretched from one canine tooth to another.

Then it stopped. It closed its mouth and retreated from the window. It looked down the road and ran back to the tree line to join the rest of its pack. Penny hesitated then jumped up and wound the window shut. She was too exhausted to think why the wolf gave up when it had won the fight, she was just thankful it did.

She knocked the lever by the steering wheel and the windscreen wipers engaged, pushing off the collecting snow from the glass. When the view of the road became clear, she saw two headlights approaching. Coming towards them slowly. They could see her; they could see the car. She was saved.

CHAPTER 12.

The family decided to stay the night. The nurses don't normally allow it but because the chances of Heather making it through the night were so slim, they bent the rules this time. Benny was happy sleeping in his pushchair which doubled as a Moses basket, Jack was given an old camp bed that was used by the night staff. Penny had the choice of the chair or the floor with a few cushions for a mattress. She chose the chair. It was big enough for her to curl up in, so she would manage.

Heather had come round for a while just after dinner. She even smiled and laughed a little which brought Penny out of her shell. It was almost like old times. Almost. Penny then played with Benny on the floor, while Jack and Heather had some time to talk alone before bed. Penny could hear plenty of gentle sobbing and lots of 'I love you so much', 'I don't know what I'll do without you.' She found it strange that it seemed to be her mum comforting her dad more than the other way round. It was her that was dying, not him.

Jack got Benny settled in his Moses basket, he sang 'Oh, you pretty things' because Heather wasn't strong enough. The evening had taken it out of her and she was already fast asleep. The nurse offered Heather a shot of morphine that she reluctantly accepted. She had wanted to keep a clear head whilst Penny was there but the pain was too much. She was strong enough to give them one final kiss before her eyes closed for the night. Possibly forever, Penny thought.

Penny curled up on the chair with a blanket, something that had been crocheted by a previous resident. The thought of that freaked her out a little, but she got her head round it and felt herself dozing just fine. Benny was sound asleep, Jack was tossing and turning for a while but then he stopped, and Penny could hear gentle rumbling coming from him as he snored. Sleep just wouldn't come for Penny. She tossed and turned, wondering how different things were going to be after tonight. She made plans in her head of how she could help dad out with things that she knew how to do from watching her mum. She could wash the pots, change Benny's nappy, make cereal for everyone on a morning. She could help out, hopefully fill some of the void and take some of the pressure from her dad.

'Psst. Penny.' A voice whispered behind her.

Penny lifted her head from the cushioned arm of the chair and looked round. The room was dark but the glow of the moon through the window lit it up enough for her to see. Her mum was looking at her smiling.

'Come get in bed with me.' She pulled the covers down. Penny shifted from the chair and cautiously got in the small bed with her mum, conscious of hurting her with an accidental kick or knee. She didn't know how much she needed the hug until it came. Heather put both arms around Penny and held her tight. She kissed Penny's head and stroked her hair for the longest time.

'Why are you dying?' Penny asked eventually, her tears soaking into her mum's pyjamas.

'Because of this awful, awful disease.'

Penny sniffed. 'Why didn't the doctors make you better with the medicine? It works for other people, why not you?'

Heather took in a deep, shuddering breath. 'Because sweet heart, I first got this disease when Ben was in my tummy. And if I had used the medicine that the doctors wanted me to have, Benny wouldn't have been born.'

Penny thought for a moment. 'But you knew that you wouldn't have died if you had the medicine earlier?' All these questions had been simmering at the surface of Penny's head for so long. For some reason, now that her mum was dying, she found it easier to ask them. Maybe the dark helped too, it made it feel as though it was a dream.

'Then we wouldn't have Benny. Could you imagine a world without Benny?'

Penny could hear the smile in her mum's voice as she said that. Penny gave that some thought and decided she couldn't.

'I can't imagine a world without you either though.' Her crying became sobs then and Heather squeezed her until all of her muscles screamed in pain, the morphine would drip again any moment but the pain was worth the feeling of comforting her daughter one last time.

'I don't want you to go. I hate this disease.' Penny added.

Heather cupped Penny's face. 'You have a fantastic father and a wonderful little brother. You'll all have each other. You'll learn that as long as you have each other, you can get through anything. You'll need to look out for Benny, your dad too, a little bit, although he'll mainly be ok. But every now and then, he might need a hug from you. Tell him he's doing a good job from time to time to. We like that, us parents.'

Penny nods and her throat starts to hurt from crying.

'You, were the greatest, most wonderful daughter I could have ever asked for.'

Penny squeezed her mum and felt how bony she had become.

Heather used her last bit of strength to grip her tightly again, hiding how much the movement hurt her.

'I love you mum.'

'I love you, penny. My pretty thing.' Heather stroked Penny's hair away from her face and began to sing, looking into her eyes. 'Oh, you pretty things.'

They hold each other for a long time, until exhausted, they both fall asleep in the bed.

When Penny is woken by her dad the next morning, her mum is dead.

CHAPTER 13.

The car came to a stop just short of being parallel with the freezing ice box that was now Penny's car. Penny watched through the windshield. She couldn't see the driver, the headlights were on full beam, she had to squint when looking in that direction. Tentatively, she waved. No one got out of the car, it just sat there, engine running and smoke billowing from the exhaust pipe, drifting up into the darkness above.

'Help.' She said, her voice hoarse from screaming for so long as the wolf attacked her. 'Help.' She said again, trying to be louder and failing.

Nothing happened for what felt like an eternity, the clock however told her it had only been five minutes. Then the car door opened and a leg appeared. A great black boot hit the snow, followed shortly by a second one. A man stood from the car and shut the door. He pulled on his belt to bring his trousers up an inch, then grabbed his crotch as if to readjust himself. Penny struggled to see any facial features because of the brightness of the car's headlights. He was a big man, bigger than her dad, who had been six-foot when they measured themselves on the door frame back home. The home she was desperate to see again. The man was wide too, Penny could make out his large hanging belly from his silhouette as he walked in front of the high beams. He approached the car with no obvious sign of urgency. He stood at the side of the car, his head above the open window. Penny could make out his shirt now, a white shirt with old crusted sauce stained on his top, probably from eating whilst driving. Her dad did the same. The man's face appeared, he had a great big wiry beard and several scratches above his right eye. His eyes were so dark brown they looked to be black. He stared at her, making her feel uncomfortable. Neither of them said anything, just looked at each other, as if weighing each other up. She was wandering if it was all a dream, but she didn't know what he was thinking. He didn't smell of beer, and he didn't look tired.

'Are you the man from the lodge?' Penny said, breaking the silence. 'Did you get my dad's message?'

The man nodded. 'Sure. Why not.' He looked around him, taking in the surroundings. He looked out into the woods but didn't notice the wolves. Penny couldn't see their yellow eyes either. 'Where's your dad?' He said and sucked on his bottom lip.

Penny nodded out the back window. 'He got hit by a car. He's dead.'

The man noticed Benny for the first time and raised his eyebrows. Without saying a word, he went over to where Jack laid in the road. He kicked the snow that had gathered on top of him, then nudged the body with his boot. Penny watched as the man knelt down and put his fingers on to Jack's neck. He came back to the window and leant his elbows on the door.

'He ain't dead. Close, hasn't got long left I'd say.'

He's alive? Penny couldn't believe what the man had said. She saw in her dad's eyes that there was nothing there.

'He's not dead?' She asked.

'Not yet. He's in bad shape though.'

'You have to help him, get him out of the cold!' Penny was frantic, she felt sick with guilt that she had left her dad out in the road all night.

'Oh I will, don't you worry about that. I'm going to help your dad but first I need to get you guys safe and warm.' Like he had flicked a switch, his voice was now lighter and friendlier. 'I've got a blanket in the car, let's get you wrapped up and warm. You must be freezing.' He smiled, it didn't look natural on him, but at least he was trying to make her comfortable. Penny felt a sudden surge of relief that the nightmare was over.

The man came back with a great big fluffy blanket. He opened the driver's door. Penny climbed over. She looked back at Benny.

'Don't worry, I'll come back for him.' The man said and gestured for her to get in the blanket as he held it wide with outstretched arms. She did. He wrapped it around her, she held her hands to her chest and he pulled it so tight it crushed the air out of her lungs. She didn't say anything because the uncomfortable feeling was outweighed by the sensation of being warm.

'Let me carry you.' The man picked her up and carried her to the car. 'What happened to your shoes?'

'An animal.' Was all she could say.

'Jeez. You really have been through it tonight.'

Penny looked over the man's wide shoulders back at where her dad laid and saw his arm move. She wanted to cry right then but was too exhausted.

The man put her in the back seat and buckled her in. He pulled on the belt so it kept her held in the seat tightly. She tried to tell him it was too tight but before she had chance, he shut the door. She'd tell him when he came back with Benny.

The warmth of the mans car tingled her face as the cold began to disappear. Something crusty on the blanket scratched at her chin. She shook her head to try and get it away, then she realised the patch of crust was too big to get away from. She watched through the windscreen. It was a big car, she noticed looking round. There were two gear sticks, one had 4X4 in big bold letters on it. The scene that had been her nightmare was lit up perfectly by the car's headlights. The man walked past the car where Benny slept and crouched down by her dad. He began routing through his pockets. Penny leant forward, watching on confused, trying to figure out what the man was doing. He must be checking for ID, a phone number. Maybe putting him in the recovery position. She felt stupid for not doing that herself. She watched the man pull out her dad's wallet, take out a small bundle of cash and throw the wallet away. He stopped briefly to look in the car window at Benny. She could see Benny waking up. He looked around expecting to see Penny but she wasn't there. Penny started to get anxious for Benny to get in the car so he knew they were safe. Something wasn't right.

The man twiddled his fingers in a wave at Benny. He had a great big smile on his face as he did so. Benny stared back at the man, his face straight and concerned. Then the man walked away back towards his own car. Penny felt panic surge through her chest making her heart pound relentlessly.

'Hey no, what are you doing?' She shouted; her throat so sore it felt like burning. 'You can't leave him.

You need to help my dad, he's freezing!'

The man got in the driver's seat; his door remained open. He sniffed inwards so his snot curdled to the back of his throat and he spat outside. He leant back and looked at Penny.

'You're not going to give me any trouble, are ya?' he said.

'What are you doing?! You can't leave them!' Penny pleaded.

The man laughed as he said: 'I don't have any use for little boys, darling. It's pretty things like you I like to take home.' He laughed loudly, when he spread his mouth open wide, she could see his teeth were all filled with black rot.

She couldn't understand what was happening, why would the man from the lodge do this...Then she realised. This wasn't the man from the lodge. She had asked him if he was and he just said 'Sure, why not.' The voice of the news reporter played back in her mind: *nine-year-old girl found murdered, a man driving a 4X4, girl raped and strangled, DNA of the attacker has been found under her finger nails, most likely from a defensive struggle.* Penny looked around, the back seat was covered in dark sticky patches, the crusty patch on the blanket was the same colour, the same as the drops on the mans t-shirt. It was blood. The scratches above his eye were from the dead girl he had raped and murdered.

'No!' Penny screamed and began shaking violently, trying to free herself.

'Sit still you little bitch!' The man shut his door and put the car in drive.

He set off going forward.

'No!' Penny looked out of her window and saw Benny crying, looking at her as she passed by. 'Benny!' She screamed. She shook from side to side. The blanket began to stretch and come loose. She got one arm out. She undid her belt which relieved the pressure on her chest.

'Stop that!' The man shouted over his shoulder. Just then, the car jumped in the air as it ran over something in the road.

'Dad!' Penny screamed. She pulled on the blanket with her free hand and it fell off. She pulled on the door handle and the door opened. The man heard the woosh of the air outside and he slammed the brakes on, slamming her into the back of his seat.

His great size meant it took a second for him to push himself out of his seat and get out. Dazed from banging her head, Penny realised she had to get out then or she wasn't going to get out ever. She pulled the door handle and kicked it open. She jumped into the snow, her legs gave way and she fell face first into the floor. The snow cushioning the blow.

'Get back here!' The man shouted close behind her.

She got to her feet and looked back, he was out and chasing after her. He was unsteady on his feet, slipping in the snow as he tried to match her pace. She ran to her car and opened the driver's door. She jumped in and turned to shut the door. The man had gained on her, he was there, reaching his hand out to grab the door before she shut it. She gripped the handle in both hands and slammed it as hard as she could. She hit the central lock button at the same time he pulled on the handle. All the doors locked with an audible *'chunk'* sound. Her door was open an inch. The man smiled, and pulled it open. She grabbed the handle and tried in vain to pull it shut again, but the man was far bigger and far stronger. He yanked the door so hard she flew out of the car and into the snow.

Benny began screaming: 'Penn-ee! Penn-ee!'

The man looked down on Penny, his face contorted with anger and rage.

'I normally keep you girls for a while before I'm finished. I think I'll make an exception with you, you fucking brat!' He kicked her in the ribs, sending her a foot into the air. The breath was kicked out of her, she tried to suck more air in but couldn't, every breath felt like she was breathing fire.

The man kicked her again, this time in the leg, then the buttocks. She was screaming in pain. Her breathing was laboured, the doctor who would later examine her would find five broken ribs and a punctured lung.

Penny laid on her back, looking up at the dark sky. The snowflakes looked like falling stars as they came towards her. She saw her mum's face. Whether it was coming from the radio or not, she wasn't sure, but she thought she could hear her mums sweet voice singing 'Oh, you pretty things.' She smiled, and knew that everything was going to be ok. Her mum was watching over her. She wouldn't let her suffer. Penny would be back with her mum soon. A peace drifted over her that blocked out every sound and smell. All the pain numbed away. The falling snow seemed to take longer to hit her, as if time had slowed down. The man appeared in her line of vision. He said something, she didn't know what. Then he raised his boot so it hovered over her face. The entire time he looked as though he was shouting, spit flew from his mouth and his brow was creased with rage.

His shouting must have affected his hearing, like Penny's was affected. Because he didn't hear the wolf. The first they both knew of the wolf's presence was when it leapt over Penny's broken and bruised body and sank its teeth into the man's throat. Blood sprayed out so far and so high, it doused the snow all the way to his truck with splatters of red dots.

Time snapped back and so did Penny's senses. The silent night air was filled with the screams of a man choking as his own blood filled his windpipe. The barks and snarls of the wolf no longer filled Penny with fear but relief. She rolled on to her front and began crawling towards her car and her crying brother. She looked over her shoulder. The man was no longer screaming. The wolf was feasting on the man, his throat now gone, soon his face would be gone too and the police would have to use his dental records to identify him. His eyes looked towards Penny, but they were the blank eyes of a dead man.

Penny made it to the car and shut the door. Benny stopped crying when he saw Penny. His lip was out and tears stained his cheeks, but he was glad to see her. She could tell. Penny forced herself into a seating position. She looked out of the window, and saw the wolf eating its dinner, finally getting the live meal it had craved. The two sets of yellow eyes in the woods looked on, and then came out into the light. It was two smaller wolves. The big wolf was their mother, Penny realised. A mother trying to feed her pups.

The radio crackled and just when Penny expected to hear David bowie, it went dead.

Penny sat back in her seat, the only sound she could hear was the faint growling coming from the feeding wolves outside and the faint sobbing of her brother behind her. She began to laugh. Hysterical, exhausted laughter. She was remembering why her dad had arranged to bring them here. They had spoke of it on the way. She had always wanted to go to Loch Ness, to see if they could see the Loch Ness monster that was a legend the whole world over. When she said, "*We're going to find Nessie!?*'

Dad replied: '*Don't get your hopes up though. Many have tried and nearly all have failed. But we can certainly have a good look whilst we're there. Who knows, the monster might find us.*'

The monster had found them alright. She thought and laughed some more.

CHAPTER 14.

Nancy Broden woke that morning at five a.m. Which was strange for her because she always slept until seven, especially on cold winter days. For some reason, she just couldn't get back off. Later that night when she thought about how she was wide awake so early, she'll put it down to fate or a helping hand guided by some divine entity.

So she got up, made a cup of tea and headed into the living room. The answer machine flashed a number 1, so she pressed play. It was the voice of a man who sounded desperate. A guest who had rented out the lodge by the Loch, he'd got stuck not far from where she was. She put down her tea and shouted at her husband to get ready, they had an emergency. When they got there, they couldn't believe what they saw. The man used his satellite phone to call for the police and ambulance, and then he began using his truck's snow plough to clear the road for them to get up. Nancy stepped over the remains of what had been a man only hours before, his flesh had been ripped form his bones, several of which were missing. Large paw prints were in the snow leading away from the body and into the woods. They looked to be too big to be a domestic dog, but there were no wolves left in Scotland, hadn't been for centuries. She then found another man in the road. His wallet was next to him, she got a look at his ID and realised then that he was the paying guest. She felt the urge to vomit but managed to suppress it. Her husband, Hank, came back up the hill having pushed all the snow off the road for the best part of two miles until he reached the main, gritted road, and then turned back.

'It's awful hank. He's dead.'

Hank scratched his head, looking down at the body they now knew to be Jack. Hank's eyes went wide. 'Nancy, his fingers.'

Nancy forced herself to look down and saw Jack's fingers twitching. 'Oh my God, he's alive!'

'What about the children?'

Nancy's face dropped. The booking was for a man and two children. They had to set up the travel cot in the smaller bedroom ready for when they arrived. She turned to the car that was covered with a thick layer snow and tried the handle. It was locked. She wiped the snow from the windows, cupped her hands and looked through. The glass was frosted and it took her a moment to make out what was inside. She could see a young boy, his head flopped in front of him.

Dead?

She couldn't tell.

Next to him was a little girl, battered and bruised.

Nancy focused through the frosted glass, trying to see if she could see signs of breathing. She knocked on the window and neither of them stirred.

'Oh my God!' She said, getting frantic.

She hit the window again, this time with her fist as hard as she could. The girls eye lids flickered; she opened her eyes. A small trickle of blood fell from the side of her mouth as she smiled.

CHAPTER 15.

The doctors gave Penny an X-ray. She was incoherent when they first found her, all she could say was Benny, who they assumed was her kid brother, and 'my dad's not dead. My dad's not dead.' They patched her up, fixed her punctured lung and set all of her broken bones. She was given a mild sedative that would help her sleep. She had been resistant on that front, not wanting Benny to be out of her sight at any point.

Benny was assessed and given a full bill of health, minus a very minor case of hypothermia. Doctors were told by Nancy that when she found them, the girl was sat in a t-shirt, her coat and jumper were wrapped around the boy keeping him warm. Nancy was able to give the police the families personal details that Jack had given when he made the booking. 'He was so excited on the phone when he booked. He said his little girl had always wanted to go searching for the Loch Ness monster. We thought it was so sweet we put a Nessie cuddly toy on her bed as a welcome gift.'

The police thanked Nancy for her help and would keep her informed on any updates.

'Thank you, officers. Such an awful thing to happen. Those roads can be so dangerous at night.'

'Especially when people don't know them. You might not have heard, but three miles further on, we found a truck in a ditch. The driver dead, died instantly. Apparently, they could smell the booze on him as soon as they opened the door. They're thinking he was the one who ran over the father.' The officer checks his notes,

'Jack Thompson. Hit and run, leaving those poor kiddies alone. Well, I guess he got a quick dose of karma didn't he.'

'Awful.' Nancy said shaking her head. 'Will he survive? Jack, I mean.'

'It's touch and go at the minute. He was out in the cold for a long time, hit by two cars and lost a lot of blood. It looks like an animal tried to eat him; half his fingers are missing. If he pulls through, it'll be nothing short of a miracle.'

'Any idea on the identity of the other body that was there? Or what the hell could have don't that to him?'

'No mam. Nothing yet, his Land Rover is being swept by forensics now, in an unrelated case. As for what did it…' The officer leaned in. 'Between you and me? I haven't got a clue what could have done that to a man. It was like he'd been attacked by some kind of monster.'

Nancy made a jittery sound a recoiled in revulsion. 'Stop it, it gives me the creeps.' She said and closed her eyes to get rid of the horrible image it brought up. 'Thank you, again. I hope you get hold of some family to come and watch after the children.'

***

The forensic unit came back with what the police had suspected when they came across the scene. The man who had been mauled by an unidentified woodland creature; was the paedophile-child killer they had been looking for. In his Land Rover they found traces of blood from the Nine-year-old girl they had found the previous day, along with the blood of two other children. One of which, was the missing Clare Halliday.

CHAPTER 16.

The man's name was Clive Hunt. He owned an old stone cottage in the Scottish Highlands, not far from where he was found. Police think he had been laying low all day, and waiting until night fall to drive home to lower his chances of being detected. It would have worked too, if he didn't stop. All killers get complacent. Clive had spread his attacks out, picking up children from different areas of the country and leaving their bodies in places with no correlation to where they were snatched from or where he lived. His greed and lust for torture was his downfall, the press said. If he hadn't have tried to strike when an opportunity was presented in front of him, he would be sat at home now, plotting his next murder.

***

His cottage was well hidden behind a line of trees and hawthorn hedges. The police made their way up the hill. A line of armed officers approached first, unsure if Clive acted alone or not. A precautionary measure. When they cleared the area, they sent in the dog unit. The dogs sniffed all around the house for traces of blood, drugs, weapons, anything. Most rooms came up with nothing. The man was a monster, but a tidy one. Every room looked to have been wiped down regularly, with nothing out of place. In his bedroom, where he had a set of pine dressers, matching wardrobe and bedside tables, they found a pair of girl's bloody knickers in his bedside drawer. Downstairs was spotless, the kitchen looked as though it had never been cooked in. The fridge was empty but the freezer was full of ready meals. They went out of the back door and into the back garden. What would have been lawn at one point was concreted over. The yard was ten metres in length and surrounded in a ten-foot-high solid wooden fence. The area towards the back was caged. Metal wire supported by a wooden frame formed a cube. Inside was a shed. On the floor was two dog bowls, one filled with food, the other had the left overs of a ready meal. The police dogs barked wildly as they got closer to the cage, barking and yelping as if in pain, they tried to turn and run the other way. They began to writhe so much the officers abandoned the effort and went in without the dogs. As they opened the door, they noticed bite marks around where a dead bolt lock had been ripped out of the wood, looking as though something had fought it's way out of the cage. The officer leading the way looked at the fence at the side of the courtyard and saw claw marks all the way up to the top of the fence. What the officers were only just realising as they walked into the cage, was that the whole of the backyard was covered with two feet of snow. Yet in the cage, it was all melted away. Great piles of dog shit were dotted everywhere, as well as smaller human faeces in the back corner. The leading officer opened the shed. He was expecting to open it up and fight torture devices, deviant sex toys, maybe even a treasure trove of perverted images and videos. Instead, he found a stairwell. He made his way down the stairs. He didn't need to find a light switch as a dim bulb was glowing down there. When he reached the bottom of the stairs, he opened the door on his left. Inside was a bedroom, a dirty mattress stained with faeces and blood laid on a concrete floor. Shelves were full of sex toys, cable ties, whips and chains. A video camera set up on a tripod in one corner. The smell made the officer gag, he struggled to keep the contents of his stomach down. It smelt of raw sewage mixed with rot and damp. His nostrils stung and his eyes watered. He coughed and wretched into his hand before moving forward. He gave the room a final glance then turned back for the door.

He stopped in the thresh hold when he heard a faint rustle behind him.

'Hello?' He said, feeling as though he was going crazy. The hairs on the back of his neck stood up and his hand drifted to the taser gun on his belt. 'Is someone there? This is the police.'

A small cough came from behind the side table.

'Show yourself.' The officer demanded shining his torch in the direction of the sound. A small dirt covered hand appeared out of the darkness. Followed by a face, swollen and misshapen from countless beatings. The girl wore rags, her legs were covered in her own waste and dried blood.

'Heaven help us.' The officer said.

CHAPTER 17.

The impact from the first car had fractured Jack's skull, causing a swelling on the brain that kept him in a coma for the first six weeks. While he slept the doctors pumped him full of antibiotics to counteract the pneumonia, performed an operation to reduce the swelling and stop the bleeding in his skull. When that was completed, they knew his chances of survival had improved. Where the murderer, now known as Clive Hunt, had ran him over, two of Jack's vertebra were broken and disjointed. Had Jack been conscious when Clive ran him over, the pain would have knocked him out cold again. When the brain showed no signs of haemorrhaging, they operated on his spine, realigning the vertebra and setting him in a full cast to keep him still. When Penny asked if he could wake up, the doctors said it was better to keep him sleeping for now, to let his back heal. Penny had been so convinced that her dad was dead when she saw him laid out in the road, that the idea of him walking and talking and hugging her again seemed like nothing but a dream, a childish fantasy that would never happen in the real world. It was when the doctor told her to think positive, that she thought about her mum. Heather wouldn't give up so easily, so neither would she. She would think positive. After all, had that night's events not shown her that you can survive against the odds? A ten-year-old girl, left alone with a toddler during a torrential snow storm halfway up a Scottish mountain, had been able to survive, not only the cold, but attacks from wolves and an attempted kidnap from a murderous paedophile. By rights, she should be dead. She felt as though she had no right to survive all of that with nothing more than hypothermia, a tooth hole in her foot and a few cracked ribs. She kept thinking of only positive outcomes. Her uncle Adam came up from London to watch over her and Benny. They were able to stay in the lodge for however long it took. Adam was different, plagued by the disease known as pessimism, he kept persisting that Penny should prepare herself for the worst. Telling her only a miracle could bring her dad back. Even if he lived, the chances of him being as he was before were astronomical with the brain damage he suffered as severe as it was. Penny nodded along, told him she understood, but secretly told herself that her dad would be fine. He'd change, just as he changed after mum died, but he'd still be her dad and he'd look after them all. Finally, her positivity was rewarded.

Jack came out of the coma; his first word was 'Penny.' Followed quickly by, 'Ben...'

The doctors were astounded at his level of coherence, they asked him questions and he answered them. What was his name, what year was it, his address? He answered them all, he recounted is version of events briefly before growing increasingly irate when his children had still not been brought to him. The doctors gave him a mild sedative, nervous that he would wrench his still healing spine. Although they had noticed his feet moving and his knees bending as he began to writhe around in frustration.

Penny walked in with Benny walking by her side holding her hand. Jack sat up and winced at the jolt of pain that shot through his skull.

'My babies.' He said and began to cry. They ran to him, climbed the chair by his bedside and hugged him tightly.

'I knew you'd be OK. I knew it!' Penny cried.

Adam stood in the doorway of the hospital room with tears standing in his eyes and his mouth spread open with shock.

'What happened to you? Nobody's telling me anything.' Jack said.

Penny told him everything that happened to her whilst he had been unconscious. She told him how sorry she was, that she thought he was dead, otherwise she never would have left him there. He reassured her that she did the right thing, that looking after Benny was the priority and she had done amazingly.

'I think mummy was watching over us. Keeping us safe.' Penny said.

'I think you might be right.' Jack smiled and held his children close to him.

CHAPTER 18.

It was three months after that reunion when Jack finally managed to walk on his own again. He was released from hospital and Adam had bought a plane ticket to take him and the kids back home. Before the flight, the owners of the holiday lodge, Nancy and Hank, told Jack he could have that weekend in the lodge with his children. He accepted.

Spring was in the air and the sun was warm, even so far into the North of Scotland. Penny was stood by the edge of the Loch with Benny, each of them throwing stones, trying to skim them along the waters surface with their uncle Adam, who had decided to stay on in case Jack struggled. Jack was sat on the veranda of the lodge, nursing his still aching back and enjoying a fresh pot of coffee when a knock on the door disturbed him. He got up from his chair, grimacing and groaning, the pains were easing everyday but they were still there. He thought he'd most likely always feel them, even when they were gone.

He answered the door to see a man he'd never met. The man stood there on the verge of an emotional breakdown or so it looked like to Jack.

'Can I help you?' Jack asked, keeping a hand firmly on the door knob ready to slam it shut.

'You don't know me, and I don't know you. But what I do know is that were it not for you and your family, my family would still be broken.'

Jack furrowed his brow and kept his stare on the man in front of him. 'Who are you?' he said eventually.

'My name is Roy Halliday, Clare Halliday's father.'

***

They stepped inside. Jack filled another mug with coffee for Roy and they sat on the veranda looking out on Penny and Benny laughing and playing.

'I can't begin to tell you how grateful we are for you and your kids. Were it not for you, Clare would still be getting tortured by that man.' He sipped his coffee before the breaking of his voice turned into a sob. 'I suppose in a way she is. She'll never forget it. She wakes up at night screaming, screaming with sheer terror because her nightmares are so vivid. It's like she's back there. Back in that stinking hole being put through all that pain. She doesn't trust men, even doctors, even me. Which breaks my heart more than I can tell you.'

'It must be hard.'

'I keep asking myself, "why her?" you know? He killed all those other girls but left my Clare alive, why? But then I suppose it doesn't really matter, does it? You can drive yourself crazy thinking like that.'

'How is she coping being back?'

'She's adjusting. It's awful of me to say but, she doesn't seem like my Clare anymore. She's changed and I know that it would be naive of me to think she'd go back to being the same girl after everything but... She doesn't smile anymore. She's stopped crying throughout the day over the little things, and has started trusting us enough that she'll get naked to have a shower with the door locked, but she doesn't smile. She watches TV, sat on the sofa across the room from us, just glaring at the TV. I don't even know if she's taking in what she's watching, she has no reactions to it.' Roy paused and wiped his face. 'I don't know why I'm telling you all of this. Probably because it's only down to you and your children that she's still alive. I guess I want someone to tell me that things will go back the way they were.'

Jack looked over at Penny running around with Benny. They were laughing so heartily together Jack couldn't help but smile. He stroked at the new hair he had grown around his face as he thought on those last words.

'About two years ago, after Penny's mum died, Penny became a shell of the girl she used to be. She had been so confident and chatty, if there was someone to listen, she'd be talking. She introverted. She kept her head down, did her school work, told the psychiatrist's what they wanted to hear so they would tell me she was doing well, she's clever like that.' Jack paused, then scratched his beard before continuing.

I'm ashamed to say that I'm only just realising now, that I don't think I've heard her laugh in all that time. She's giggled at the odd thing on a movie or one of my stupid dad jokes that struck a chord. But she never properly laughed. It's amazing how affected people can be on the inside, without showing any indication of that suffering on the outside. She was never in trouble at school, she never lashed out or misbehaved, never rebelled against me. If anything, she took on more responsibility, doing jobs round the house her mother used to do, setting off the washer, folding laundry, looking after her baby brother when I was busy.

She had to grow up quick. I know now that when her mum died, it was as though Penny's childhood died as well. What we went through up on that mountain, unpicked a stitch inside her that had fastened all of that away. It'll still take some time, but she'll get there. She's enjoying life again and now I can see it. I see what I didn't see before. I see how much pain she had been in just by seeing the joy in her now. I feel full of shame in myself and pride in her because she was able to work out all the pain and come to peace with everything, without me. They say kids are more robust than we think, I just think they hide it better.

So when you ask me if things will go back the way they were, I'll say no. Things will never be the same for any of you, but things will get better. As time goes by, little by little, that darkness that is hiding your daughters smile will get brighter, and one day, it will become so bright that you will see that smile through what was once only darkness, pain and misery. You'll still remember, you'll still be haunted by it, but it'll be better. You'll all process it and file it into the back of your mind where you can bring it out every once in a while, but one day when you bring it back, it'll be to say, "We survived that." And instead of bringing you terror and nightmares, it'll bring you strength. Until the day comes where the brightness shines so brightly that the darkness is hardly there at all, and then you'll see the happiness in her face and you'll hear the laughter in her voice. Your family will never be the same Roy. But they will be happy again.' Jack held up a finger and the sound of Penny's laughter carried across to them from the side of the Loch where they stood throwing stones into the water. 'That's the sound of happiness.'

CHAPTER 19.

Penny saw her dad talking to the man back at the lodge. She didn't know who he was, but she could tell by the way he held himself that he was no threat. She felt she had a better perception for spotting danger now.

Benny and Adam had run off down the shore line of the great Loch Ness in search of flat stones to skim. Penny looked out over the water, the sun danced and shimmered on the ripples as the water lapped soothingly towards her. She felt an incredible peace wash over her, the breeze felt like delicate fingers brushing through her hair. She thought of her mother and smiled. Looking out over the shimmering water, hearing the sound of Benny's laughter and the touch of her mother's fingers through her hair, she thought this was closest she'd ever been to heaven.

She was brought out of her daze when she saw a sleek black shape break out of the surface of the water far off in the distance before disappearing.

'Did you see that?' Her uncle Adam said. 'Or were my eyes playing tricks.'

Penny smiled. 'Just your eyes playing tricks uncle.'

Oh, you pretty things echoed in her mind as if her mother was singing it in her ear.

*There's no monsters her*e.

END

Printed in Great Britain
by Amazon